Marriage Certificate

Let it be known that as of
September 2001, Jayne Pembroke,
the red-headed beauty of 20 Amber Court,
Apt. 1C, is legally bound to Erik Randolph,
one of Youngsville, Indiana's most eligible
bachelors, in holy matrimony. Both parties
will live in wedded bliss, for a period of one year,
until the terms of Erik's inheritance have been
met. They will mutually agree to ignore the
overwhelming attraction that has been there since
Erik's spontaneous proposal, as well as the desire
to be more than just an in-name-only couple.
Jayne will take Erik's name and hope that, in turn,
her new husband does not take her heart. In the
event that something like *true love* develops, this
contract will become null and void so that they
may draw up a new certificate based on matters
of the heart.

Dear Reader,

Welcome to Silhouette Desire, where you can indulge yourself every month with six passionate, powerful and provocative romances! And you can take romance one step further.... Look inside for details about our exciting new contest, "Silhouette Makes You a Star."

Popular author Mary Lynn Baxter returns to Desire with our MAN OF THE MONTH when *The Millionaire Comes Home* to Texas to reunite with the woman he could never forget. Rising star Sheri WhiteFeather's latest story features a *Comanche Vow* that leads to a marriage of convenience...until passionate love transforms it into the real thing.

It's our pleasure to present you with a new miniseries entitled 20 AMBER COURT, featuring four twentysomething female friends who share an address...and their discoveries about life and love. Don't miss the launch title, *When Jayne Met Erik*, by beloved author Elizabeth Bevarly. The scandalous Desire miniseries FORTUNES OF TEXAS: THE LOST HEIRS continues with *Fortune's Secret Daughter* by Barbara McCauley. Alexandra Sellers offers you another sumptuous story in her miniseries SONS OF THE DESERT: THE SULTANS, *Sleeping with the Sultan.* And the talented Cindy Gerard brings you a touching love story about a man of honor pledged to marry an innocent young woman with a secret, in *The Bridal Arrangement.*

Treat yourself to all six of these tantalizing tales from Silhouette Desire.

Enjoy!

Joan Marlow Golan

Joan Marlow Golan
Senior Editor, Silhouette Desire

Please address questions and book requests to:
Silhouette Reader Service
U.S.: 3010 Walden Ave., P.O. Box 1325, Buffalo, NY 14269
Canadian: P.O. Box 609, Fort Erie, Ont. L2A 5X3

WHEN JAYNE MET ERIK

ELIZABETH BEVARLY

Published by Silhouette Books

America's Publisher of Contemporary Romance

Special thanks and acknowledgment are given
to Elizabeth Bevarly for her contribution
to the 20 AMBER COURT series.

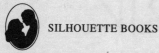 SILHOUETTE BOOKS

ISBN 0-373-76389-1

WHEN JAYNE MET ERIK

Copyright © 2001 by Harlequin Books S.A.

Visit Silhouette at www.eHarlequin.com

Printed in U.S.A.

Books by Elizabeth Bevarly

ELIZABETH BEVARLY

is an honors graduate of the University of Louisville and achieved her dream of writing full-time before she even turned thirty! At heart, she is also an avid voyager who once helped navigate a friend's thirty-five-foot sailboat across the Bermuda Triangle. Her dream is to one day have her own sailboat, a beautifully renovated older-model forty-two-footer, and to enjoy the freedom and tranquillity seafaring can bring. Elizabeth likes to think she has a lot in common with the characters she creates, people who know love and life go hand in hand. And she's getting some firsthand experience with motherhood, as well—she and her husband have a seven-year-old son, Eli.

For Joan Marlow Golan,
Gail Chasan
And Allison Lyons.
With many thanks.

One

Jayne Pembroke was *not* having a good day.

She began it by oversleeping, a development made even worse by the fact that she awoke from the most wonderful dream she'd had in a long, long time—a development made even worse when she confronted the reality to which she did, eventually, awake. Because in her dream, Jayne had had company. Really nice company, too, in the form of a handsome, dark-haired, dark-eyed stranger, who had been performing the most wondrous—and erotic—activities with her.

At least, Jayne *thought* they were wondrous, erotic activities. She was pretty sure they were, anyway. She did have cable TV, after all. Admittedly, though, she didn't have much personal experience with wondrous, erotic activities by which to judge…or *any* personal experience, for that matter. But whatever it was that the dark-haired, dark-eyed stranger had been doing to her in her dream, it had felt really, really good.

Her reality, on the other hand, was...not. Not wondrous. Not erotic. And certainly not good. Because in addition to being late, Jayne was, as always, alone.

When she finally did glance over at the clock and noted the time, she tumbled out of bed—literally—bonking her head on the nightstand in the process. So she kicked the nightstand in retaliation...and banged her little toe in exactly that way that made it hurt the most. Then, as she hopped on one foot toward her bathroom, Mojo, her sister Chloe's cat, whom Jayne was keeping while Chloe attended college, came gallumphing into the room—doubtless because Mojo knew Jayne would be hopping around on one foot—and tripped her. That, naturally, caused her to fall down, and in doing so she banged her knee viciously on the hardwood floor.

Things just went downhill from there.

The water in the shower was barely tepid by the time Jayne turned it on, thanks, no doubt, to the fact that everyone *else* who lived at 20 Amber Court had already had *their* showers because *they'd* awoken on time. Then the only clean shirt she was able to find did not match the only clean skirt she was able to find, and the only pair of clean panty hose she was able to find had a run in them. As a result, she was forced to don a blinding combination of raspberry top and burnt-orange skirt, along with the only belt she could find in her overly tousled closet— which, it went without saying, was chartreuse.

Not surprisingly, her hair dryer shorted out the moment she switched it on, emitting a dangerous-sounding *zzzt* coupled with the smell of something burning. Immediately she jerked the plug from the wall and dumped the appliance in the wastebasket—which overturned, spilling its entire contents across the bathroom floor.

She bit back a scream—and quite a hysterical one it had threatened to be, too—then methodically wove her long, straight, *wet,* red hair into a thick braid that fell between her shoulderblades, and ruffled her bangs dry as best she could. She swiped a bit of raspberry-colored lipstick over her mouth—at least *some*thing would match at least *part* of her clothes—and dragged a bit of neutral shadow over her violet eyes. Then she ran into the kitchen for the cup of coffee she absolutely *had* to consume in order to function as a halfway effective human being.

The good news was that the coffeemaker's timer had, amazingly, worked perfectly. The bad news was that when Jayne had filled the coffeemaker the night before, she had neglected to add any...well, coffee. So only a pot of hot water greeted her.

She bit back another one of those certain-to-be-hysterical screams—but just barely. Then, surrendering to the fact that she wouldn't be enjoying her morning cuppa today—or much of anything else, for that matter—Jayne turned her attention to the kitchen window and saw that, inescapably, it was an unusually rainy morning for the first of September. And of course, likewise inescapably, she recalled that she'd left her only umbrella at Colette Jewelry, the showroom of the highly successful Colette, Inc., where she worked as a salesclerk, the last time it had rained.

My, my, my, she thought. What else could the day possibly hold? It wasn't even 9:00 a.m.

As quickly as she could, she hurried through the rest of her morning rituals, doing her absolute best to make completely certain that nothing else went wrong. And really, not much else did go wrong. Except for when she chipped her favorite coffee mug putting it away, broke her fingernail to the quick while performing a quick search for her raincoat—which, naturally, she never found—and stepped on a pile of stray cat kibble, crushing it to a fine powder that she'd have to sweep up when she got home, because there was no way she had time to do that now.

But other than that...

She was locking her front door to apartment 1C when

the door to 1A-B, the apartment next to hers—the one belonging to her landlady—opened. It was the first thing to happen that morning that made Jayne smile. Rose Carson just inspired that kind of reaction in a person, a feeling of good cheer and well-being. She was, to put it simply, a nice lady. She'd even been the one who had helped Jayne find a job at Colette Jewelry. A friend of a friend, Rose had told Jayne, had mentioned an opening in the jewelry store. Jayne had been hired for the salesclerk position the day she had applied.

Judging by Rose's short, dark hair that was just starting to go gray, by the laugh lines that crinkled her dark eyes, and by the older woman's matronly figure, Jayne guessed her landlady's age to be somewhere in her fifties. About the same age Jayne's mother would be now, had Doris Pembroke survived the plane crash that had killed her and Jayne's father four years ago.

Even though Jayne had only lived at 20 Amber Court for a month, she felt as if she'd known Rose Carson forever. Her landlady was the kind of person who inspired immediate affection and fast camaraderie, the kind in whom one felt totally comfortable confiding. Within days of Jayne's move to the apartment building, she'd found herself revealing to Rose all the particulars of her past and current situations. About the loss of both her parents when she was eighteen, about taking on the care of her then-fourteen-year-old twin siblings, Chloe and Charlie, immediately thereafter, about sacrificing her own opportunity to attend college in order to send Chloe and Charlie instead.

Jayne didn't mind the sacrifice, though. She'd always felt responsible for the twins, even when she was a child. And she knew neither of them took her sacrifice for granted. Once her brother and sister finished college themselves in four years, she'd go back and earn her own degree. She had plenty of time, after all. She was only twenty-two, and her whole life lay stretched before her.

She was just looking forward to having a bit of stability in that life for a change. The last four years had been more than a little difficult, seeing to the needs of Charlie and Chloe and herself, making sure all three of them kept a roof over their heads and food in their bellies.

The sale of their parents' home, along with a modest life insurance settlement and social security for the twins, had afforded them the financial boost they'd needed during that time. But now that Chloe and Charlie were eighteen, the social security was gone. And college tuition for two, even with the twins' partial scholarships, was going to prove a challenge. Still, the Pembroke finances were stable and reasonably secure right now. As long as Jayne had her job at Colette Jewelry and lived within her modest budget, everything would be fine.

She hoped.

"Good morning, Jayne," Rose Carson said with a smile as she closed her own door and turned toward her newest tenant. She glanced down at her watch. "You're running a bit late, aren't you, dear?"

Jayne quelled the panic that threatened to rise again. She wasn't *that* late, she reminded herself. Thanks to all her rushing around—and skipping her morning coffee—she could still make it to work with a few minutes to spare. Maybe. If she ran the entire way. Which, of course, she would, seeing as how she had missed the bus, and it was still raining. Colette, Inc. was only ten blocks from 20 Amber Court. And if she hugged the buildings between here and there, the awnings might provide enough shelter to keep her dry. Sort of.

"A bit late, yes," Jayne conceded to her landlady. "It's been one of those mornings," she couldn't help adding with no small exasperation.

Rose nodded, clearly understanding. "Rainy days and Mondays, right?" she asked.

Jayne chuckled derisively. "Rainy days and Mondays, and broken alarm clocks and broken hair dryers, and no clean laundry and uncooperative coffeemakers, and homicidal cats and—''

Rose held up a hand, laughing. ''Say no more,'' she said. ''Oh, my. I've had a few of those days myself.''

Jayne was about to say goodbye and scuttle off when she noticed the brooch affixed to Rose's cream-colored blouse. Not quite heart-shaped and not quite triangular, it was unusual and very beautiful, encrusted with dark yellowish stones set in what appeared to be several different metals. So captivated was she by the accessory, she found herself involuntarily lifting a hand toward it.

''Your pin is so beautiful, Rose,'' she said, speaking her thoughts aloud. ''That's not topaz, though, is it?'' She glanced up after voicing her question, only to find Rose beaming at her as if Jayne had just paid her the highest compliment in the world.

''No, it's amber,'' her landlady replied. ''Amber and some precious metals.''

Jayne nodded as she touched a fingertip gently to the brooch. ''Someone must have given it to you because you live at 20 Amber Court,'' she said.

Rose smiled again, a bit sadly this time. ''No, I've had this for quite some time now. There's a rather interesting history behind it, actually.''

''You'll have to tell me about it sometime,'' Jayne said, dropping her hand back to her side. ''Sometime when I'm not running so late and having such a crummy day,'' she added when she recalled her current situation. She started to say farewell again, when Rose stopped her.

''Wait,'' her landlady said impulsively. She reached for the pin Jayne had just admired. ''Wear this today,'' she told her tenant with a cryptic little smile, her dark eyes sparkling. ''In the past, it's brought me what you might call 'good luck.' Maybe it will help get you through the rest of the day.''

Jayne expelled a single, humorless chuckle. ''The way this day has started, I have a feeling it's not going to be 'one of those days' so much as it's going to be 'one of those months.'"

"Then wear it all month, if you need to," Rose told her, unfastening the pin from her own blouse and deftly fixing it on Jayne's. With a mischievous little smile she added, "You'll know when it's time to give it back."

"Oh, I couldn't—" Jayne started to object.

"Of course you could," Rose insisted. "There," she said, patting the pin in place. "It doesn't exactly match your outfit, but…"

This time Jayne laughed in earnest. "But then my outfit doesn't exactly match much of anything, does it? Remind me if you see me later today that I have a lot of laundry to do tonight, okay?"

Rose nodded. "Will do, dear."

Jayne turned an eye to the large marble foyer of 20 Amber Court, gazing through the big glass windows at the bleak, gray day outside. Thankfully, the rain had ebbed to a scant drizzle, so she closed her eyes for a moment and willed the scant drizzle to *stay* that way, at least until she reached Colette. And then, with one more halfhearted smile for Rose, she lifted a hand in farewell.

"Good luck today!" her landlady called after her as Jayne hastened toward the front door.

"Thanks!" Jayne called back. "Something tells me I'm going to need it!"

On the other side of Youngsville, Indiana, Erik Randolph wasn't having a particularly good morning, either—though for entirely different reasons.

His own sleep the night before had been restful and dreamless, and he didn't wake up late for work. That would be because, simply put, he had no work for which to wake up late. Oh, he *could* go to work, if he wanted to—it was no secret that his father was holding a VP position for him at Randolph Shipping and Transportation. But it was also no secret that Erik wasn't much suited to work. Work required something like oh…a work ethic, for one thing. A sense of purpose for another. Or even a feeling of duty, or a desire to provide. Erik, it was commonly known, lacked all of those things. Though, it was likewise commonly known, that didn't detract from his charm one iota.

So as it stood now, his hour of waking was completely immaterial, because he would spend today as he spent every day—without any specified activities or agenda in mind. And although he awoke alone, it was because he had *chosen* to awake alone, which was his habit when he spent the night at his house.

That, of course, was because he shared his house with his parents, who were the actual owners of the house. But it wasn't because he feared discovery by said parents that caused Erik to sleep alone—in fact, the Randolph estate was so large and so spacious, one could be sharing it with the United Arab Emirates and not run into anyone for months. It was because Erik just never quite felt comfortable when he was at home. Certainly not comfortable enough to entertain anyone there.

And, anyway, entertaining was his mother's milieu. Erik was far better suited to being entertained.

In any case he didn't like to spend any more time at his parents' estate than was absolutely necessary. He wasn't sure why that was. Certainly the house was beautifully and elegantly decorated, filled with only the best that money could buy—the most luxurious Persian rugs, the finest European antiques, the most exquisite works of art. And certainly his parents and his two younger sisters were all likable enough people, and, as a family, they all got along very well. But there was something missing here. The house lacked…something. Erik wasn't quite sure what. And as a result, he was just never all that comfortable when he was at home.

It was only one of the reasons he spent so much time traveling. The other reason, of course, would be that traveling was just so much fun. And still another reason was that traveling introduced him to so many wonderful people, from so many walks of life, many of whom—the female ones, at any rate—he could share serious, monogamous relationships with, often for days on end. Jet-setting playboy, Erik had concluded a long time ago, was just about the best occupation a man could have.

Still, when he was forced to spend time at home in Youngsville, his parents' estate was more than accommodating. Even at 9:00 a.m., Erik was still clad in his burgundy silk robe and pajama bottoms, stretched out in his king-size bed, the remnants of his breakfast lying neglected now on the silver tray that Bates, the true-blue Randolph butler, had placed beside him an hour ago. And although Erik felt restless and edgy, as if he were on the brink of some vague, life-altering experience, he just couldn't quite muster the energy necessary to pull himself out of bed and go greet that experience head-on.

Really, what was the point? he asked himself, dragging an impatient hand through his overly long, dark hair. It was Monday, it was raining, and he could think of no better way to spend the day than idling about. On top of everything else, it was the first day of September, reminding him that his thirtieth birthday was this month, and that—

Suddenly, Erik understood his restlessness, his edginess, his need to go out and meet that life-altering experience head-on. His thirtieth birthday was two weeks away. Damn. This was just what he needed. He'd dedicated his entire summer to zigzagging around the globe, miring himself in denial over the fact that he would soon be thirty years old. Now, suddenly, there it was, staring him in the face. His thirtieth birthday. Only two weeks away. Fourteen days. That was all he had left to his twenties. Two lousy weeks, fourteen lousy days.

Thirty. He was about to turn thirty. God. When had *that* happened?

It wasn't so much the chronological significance of turning thirty that bothered Erik. Although he'd very much enjoyed his twenties, he didn't consider thirty to be the end of his life. On the contrary, he knew several people who were actually *in* their thirties, and they seemed to be having a surprisingly good time. Many of them even claimed that their thirties were actually *more* enjoyable than their twenties had been.

Not that Erik was quite willing to go that far, but he wasn't all that averse to turning thirty. Or, at least, he wouldn't be. Not if it weren't for the fact that he had a familial obligation he needed to meet soon. Like, by his thirtieth birthday. Like, in two weeks. Like, in fourteen days.

Fourteen lousy days.

Because within fourteen lousy days, Erik had to acquire something very specific in order to claim an inheritance, currently in trust, left to him by his paternal grandfather. Certainly it wouldn't break Erik financially if he declined the inheritance—even without his grandfather's riches, the Randolphs were an exceedingly wealthy family. But Erik's father was adamant that Erik take possession of the estate that the elder Randolph felt was his entitlement.

Damien Randolph, Erik's father, hadn't gotten along particularly well with his own father—in fact, the two men had stopped speaking to each other more than a decade ago. As a result, Grandfather Randolph had split his entire estate—his entire estate of $180 million—between Erik and his two sisters, bypassing his own son entirely.

Of course, it was all contingent on one small stipulation. Because Grandfather Randolph had feared that his grandchildren would never outgrow their notorious playboy and playgirl habits—and for good reason, too, Erik couldn't help but think now—the will stated that in order to claim their share of the estate, each would have to meet that one simple stipulation before his or her thirtieth birthday. Not that Erik's sisters had to worry about it for some time—Celeste was four years younger than Erik, and Maureen was eight years younger than he—so Erik would be the test subject. And because he *did* have a good relationship with his own father, Erik felt rather obligated to meet his grandfather's requirement, and keep in the Randolph family as much of the Randolph wealth as possible. Really, it was the least Erik could do for his father.

And hey, his share *did* amount to sixty million dollars.

It wasn't every day that a man acquired an estate that large and that secure. Grandfather Randolph had been a very wise investor. Once Erik inherited, he'd be set for life. Not that he wasn't already pretty much set right now, but a man could never be too sure.

And had he mentioned that his share did amount to sixty million dollars?

Still, there was that one simple criterion Erik was obligated to meet before he could take control of his inheritance, and he had to meet it by his thirtieth birthday. Really, it wouldn't be all that hard to do. What Erik needed to find could be found almost anywhere. He just hadn't gotten around to looking for one yet, that was all. Now that he only had fourteen days, though, he supposed he should get hopping.

But where to look first, he wondered? Did the Yellow Pages have a listing for what he needed? If he looked under *W*, would he find a section labeled Wives?

Ah, well. If not, no problem. Should he find a shortage of wives in Youngsville, he'd just pick one up somewhere else. Chicago was right across Lake Michigan and was quite a bit larger than his own community. If he couldn't find a wife here in town, then surely they had plenty of potential wives over there.

Besides, it wasn't as if he was going to have to *keep* the wife he found. Grandfather's will stated quite clearly that Erik need only remain married for one year in order to collect his inheritance. He supposed his grandfather thought that a year of settling down would be enough to *keep* Erik settled down. Grandfather Randolph had been so utterly smitten by his own wife that the thought of the marriage ending prematurely had never crossed his mind. The old man had probably thought that Erik need only spend enough time in the company of a good woman to become equally smitten himself.

In a word, Hah.

Not only was Erik much too pragmatic to believe in anything as…as…as *silly*…as romantic love, but he was also much too entrenched in his globe-trotting playboy lifestyle—not to mention he liked that lifestyle way too much—to ever abandon it. Still, he could put it on hold for a year if it meant maintaining the family status quo, couldn't he? Especially if it meant maintaining the family status quo *and* inheriting millions and millions and *millions* of dollars.

Sometimes, he thought, one just had to make a sacrifice.

Content with his decision to start wife hunting that very morning, Erik rose from his bed. As he launched himself into a full-body stretch, he began his mental shopping list, making note of all the qualities he would require in his wife. She would, it went without saying, have to be beautiful. And blond. He'd always liked blondes, so that's what he would look for in his wife. Eye color wasn't especially important, but brown eyes on a blonde were always a good thing, in his opinion. His wife would also have to be reasonably intelligent and fairly articulate. He did so dislike empty conversations. Not that she would need to expound on physics and genetics—au contraire— but knowledge of the current fashion climate would be most welcome.

Let's see, what else…? he wondered.

She would need to be demure, perhaps even coquettish, and it would be preferable if she had a mild disposition. She should be a free thinker, but open to suggestions, and she would have to have some working knowledge of the social register, not to mention the ins and outs of proper etiquette. Erik attended a lot of parties, and he expected his wife to be as comfortable in such settings as he was himself. She'd need to have a sense of style, a love of fine wine, an appreciation for the arts…

He really should start writing this down, he thought. So much to do, so little time.

A rousing clap of thunder reminded him that he would be doing it in less-than-agreeable weather, too. Still, that would only add to the challenge, wouldn't it? And Erik did appreciate challenges. Provided, of course, they weren't *too* challenging.

Then again, what could possibly be challenging about finding a wife? He was one of Youngsville's most eligible bachelors. He'd read that himself in the Sunday magazine section of the *Youngsville Gazette* not too long ago. Therefore, it must be true. He was practically a local celebrity. Any woman would jump at the chance to be his wife. He had everything to offer—good looks, wry wit, cheerful disposition, good finances, a nice home. All right, so that last was actually not his, in name. That was a minor technicality. It was still a nice part of his personal package. In fact, the only thing Erik could think of that he lacked as a potential suitor was—

A ring. An engagement ring. He'd certainly need one of those if he was going to attract the right woman. A wife would first have to be a fiancée, and he couldn't have a fiancée without the proper ring. Of course, only the finest ring would be suitable for Erik Randolph's future wife. And everyone in Youngsville, Indiana, knew where you went if you wanted to purchase the best in jewelry.

Colette, Inc.

That would be Erik's first stop on his wife-hunting safari today, he decided. He'd find just the right ring, one that was beautiful without being showy, exquisite without being ostentatious, elegant without being plain. Much like the woman he hoped to find, he couldn't helping thinking whimsically.

Yes, Colette, he was certain, would have exactly what he was looking for.

Two

By the time Jayne entered Colette Jewelers on Hammond Street, she was as wet and limp and bedraggled as a street urchin—a street urchin who had just walked eight blocks in a raging downpour, without an umbrella to shelter her from the storm. Because as soon as she had covered the first two blocks between Amber Court and Colette, the skies had opened up and dumped veritable buckets of rain down on Youngsville. It had effectively put an end to the scant drizzle Jayne had hoped would accompany her to work and had begun a deluge of biblical proportions. Not even the awnings had been able to save her after that. So now, in addition to being mismatched, she was completely wet and limp and bedraggled.

And cold, too, because the air-conditioning in the store was blasting full speed ahead, despite the inclement weather, and the chill breeze against her wet flesh and clothing raised goose bumps on her goose bumps. Although the situation was beginning to look dire, Jayne told herself to buck up. Because, after all, things couldn't possibly get any worse, could they?

Belatedly she realized that thinking such a thing completely jinxed her. Because where she normally arrived at work to find the shop in its empty, preopening state—a condition that would have afforded her an opportunity to at least *try* and tidy herself up before anyone saw her— today, the Colette Jewelry showroom played host to a good half dozen of Jayne's co-workers, who were in the shop because today was Colette employee discount day.

Oh, yes. The day was definitely going to get worse. Before it was over, Jayne, looking as bad as she had ever looked in her life, was bound to run into every last person who worked for the company. Because every last person who worked for the company worked in that very building, and virtually all of them took advantage of their twice-yearly employee discount days.

The building that housed Colette, Inc. was a massive, eight-story brick construction that comprised one full city block, located virtually at the center of Youngsville. A large showroom and shop took up the entirety of the first floor, and the corporate offices commanded the remainder of the building. The furnishings, overall, were quite luxuriant, regardless of where one might find oneself in the establishment. Rich jewel tones of varying hues darkened the walls, upon which were hung priceless works of art. Oriental rugs of equally dramatic color and design spanned the hardwood floors, and expensive pieces of sculpture filled all the spaces that weren't used up in the display of jewelry. Bright track lighting overhead made everything—especially the finely cut gems—sparkle like, well, finely cut gems.

In addition to the offices upstairs, the building housed a formal dining room for executives and an open cafeteria for the other employees. Jayne had never seen the former, but she spent most of her lunch hours in the latter. It, too, was elegantly appointed, and furnished in much the same way as the rest of the building. She assumed the executive dining room was likewise decorated.

But her favorite place in the Colette building—besides the jewelry showroom and shop, both of which she found utterly enchanting—was the lobby of the corporate offices on the second floor, where she'd gone to meet some of her co-workers on one or two occasions. Because in that lobby was the most exquisite piece of jewelry Jayne had ever seen—a single rose crafted of rubies and diamonds and emeralds. She wasn't sure what the history was behind the piece, and she'd never asked anyone at Colette. She only knew that it was lovely, and Jayne, like so many people who worked for the company, simply adored beautiful things.

Which was another reason why she felt so out of place this morning. Beautiful, she knew, was the last thing she looked today. And her co-workers mingling about the store now seemed to agree, because she could see them biting back smiles and stifling chuckles when they took in her appearance.

So much for things not getting any worse, she thought morosely. From here on out, she wasn't about to form any more observations on the state of her day. It could only lead to trouble.

She was much relieved to discover that a trio of employees standing nearest the "New Designs" showcase were women she knew well. Because, like Jayne, they lived at 20 Amber Court. And all three had obviously arrived at work on time today, because none of them resembled a limp, bedraggled street urchin in any way, shape or form—oh, no. Each of them was very well put together, sartorially speaking. Not to mention quite dry.

Lila Maxwell lived on the third floor of Jayne's apartment building and worked on the fourth floor of Colette. She was an administrative assistant to Nicholas Camden, a vice president of the company, in charge of overseas marketing. Lila was dressed today as she always was—

for success. And lots of it. Her long, dark-blond hair shone like finely tempered bronze beneath the halogen lights of the showroom, offsetting her dark-brown eyes as if they were bittersweet chocolate. Her charcoal suit was stylishly cut, hugging her curves with much affection.

She was chatting in low tones with two of Jayne's other neighbors and co-workers—Meredith Blair, who was a jewelry designer for Colette, and Sylvie Bennett, who worked as a marketing manager for the company. Meredith, as always, was dressed in her usual, nondescript style, her long beige skirt and shapeless ivory sweater doing nothing to enhance what could be a very curvy figure and truly spectacular facial features, if Meredith would only give herself a chance. Her long, reddish-brown, curly hair was, as usual, pulled tersely away from her face, held in place with a barrette that was as nondescript as her clothing.

Although she'd only known Meredith for a month, Jayne recognized her neighbor's low self-esteem and knew Meredith went out of her way to downplay her appearance in an effort to make herself invisible. Which wasn't going to work much longer, as far as Jayne was concerned, because Meredith designed some of the most beautiful jewelry Jayne had ever seen. She was sure to go far in the business. People were going to start noticing her soon. And then what would Meredith do?

Not that Jayne was in any position to criticize the other woman's style...or lack thereof. At least Meredith's clothing matched. And was dry. Glancing down at her own questionable appearance again, Jayne found herself wishing *she* could be invisible—at least for today.

Sylvie, on the other hand, despite the quiet, obviously serious conversation in which the three women were engaged, appeared to be her usual feisty self. Her expression was more intense than the other women's, as if she were gearing up for battle. Her stark black curls were swept back at her nape, her dark-brown eyes flashed fire. Coupled with her deep burgundy power suit, she appeared a formidable force indeed.

Doing her best not to make wet, squishy sounds as she walked, Jayne strode toward the group. But the three women were so wrapped up in their conversation that they didn't even notice her approach. Not until Jayne greeted them.

"G-g-g-good m-m-m-morning," she said through chattering teeth as she halted, resigned to her fate. "L-l-l-lovely m-m-m-morning, is-s-sn't it-t-t-t?"

The three women turned to her at once, opening their mouths to reply. But when they got a collective look at her, they hesitated. For one taut moment no one said a word. Then all three of her neighbors responded in unison.

"Jayne, if I'd known you were walking today, I would have offered you a lift," Sylvie told her.

"I just made it in myself before the skies opened up," Meredith added.

"You could have taken the bus with me, you know," Lila threw in for good measure.

Jayne lifted a hand to stop the flow of commentary. After all, it wasn't as if they were telling her anything she didn't already know. "I overslept, so I was running late and missed the bus," she said. "Thanks for the offer of a lift, Sylvie, but I'm sure I missed you, too. Besides, it was barely drizzling when I left home. I thought the buildings would shelter me well enough. I should have known better. It's definitely going to be one of those days—I can feel it in my bones."

Automatically, she reached for the brooch Rose Carson had pinned to her blouse earlier. "I did run into Rose, though, before I left. She insisted I wear this pin." Jayne smiled wryly as her friends leaned in for a closer look. "She said it would bring me good luck, but I don't think *anything* can improve this day. Things are only going to get worse from here. Mark my words."

There, she thought. By saying that she expected the

worst, surely things would get better. Then she immediately cursed herself, because in supposing things would get better, she had surely just jinxed herself *again.* And on top of just jinxing herself again, she'd just tried to reverse-psychology fate. And that, she was certain, was bound to be a major metaphysical no-no.

Sure enough, in response to her remark, all three of her friends exchanged curious—and clearly very anxious—glances, and Jayne got the distinct impression that things were indeed about to get worse. Again.

"What?" she demanded, her stomach clenching nervously in response to their obvious worry. "What's wrong?"

For a moment she didn't think any of them would answer her. Then, finally, Lila hastily replied, "It's just a rumor."

Oh, that didn't sound good *at all,* Jayne thought. And, just like that, all thoughts of her current state of personal discomfort immediately fled to the back of her brain. "What's just a rumor?" she asked.

This time it was Sylvie who answered. "It's about Colette," she said simply.

"What about it?" Jayne asked.

"Well," Sylvie began again, "it's like Lila said—just a rumor."

Jayne switched her gaze from one woman to the other and back again. "But what, exactly, is *it?*" she demanded more frantically. "What's wrong? Why do you all look like you're expecting the end of the world?"

"It's a hostile takeover of the company," Meredith blurted out with an artist's kind of spontaneity.

"A hostile takeover?" Jayne echoed. "What do you mean a hostile takeover? Why would anyone want to hostilely take over Colette, Inc.? It's such a nice company."

"That's why someone wants to take it over," Meredith pointed out. "Word has it that someone—and nobody seems to know who—is buying up shares of Colette in an effort to have controlling interest.''

''But that won't affect us, will it?'' Jayne asked hopefully—and probably naively, she couldn't help thinking.

''Well, there is that pesky business of our jobs,'' Sylvie said mildly. ''Hostile takeovers have a tendency to lead to downsizing, and downsizing has a tendency to cause unemployment. Oh, but hey, other than that...''

''But...but...but...'' Jayne sputtered. Unfortunately she had no idea what to say.

''Look, there's no need to panic,'' Lila said emphatically. ''It's just a rumor.''

But rumors were almost always at least grounded in truth, Jayne thought. And this one was doubtless no different. ''What happens if Colette is taken over?'' she asked. ''Hostilely or not? What *will* happen to our jobs?''

Jayne was completely ignorant when it came to all things corporate related. Although she genuinely enjoyed her job as a salesclerk, she really wasn't much interested with the workings of the business as a whole. Her familiarity with Colette, Inc., was limited to the history of the company that was common knowledge in Youngsville, what she'd heard from her neighbor co-workers, and what she'd learned herself in employee training a month ago. About how Abraham Colette, whose family had been in the jewelry business in Paris for generations, came to Youngsville from France in 1902 to start over. About how he married a local girl named Teresa and started his own branch of the company, which soon became known for having the most precious of precious gems in the most exquisite of settings.

Even during the Depression, Colette, Inc., had flourished, thanks to Carl Colette, Abraham and Teresa's son, who naturally followed in his father's footsteps, and had had the foresight to bring in investors a decade earlier. As a result, over the years, Colette had become known nationwide, even worldwide, for its unique and elegant pieces, pieces created by only the finest designers and craftspeople.

Which, Jayne thought further, probably went a long way toward explaining this hostile takeover business.

"What will happen to our jobs if someone takes over the company?" she asked again when no one offered a reply—which wasn't exactly reassuring. "I can't lose this job," she said further. "I was lucky to get it in the first place, and that was only because Rose put in a good word for me. I'm not trained to do anything. I'd never find something else that pays as well as this. I need my commissions," she added, swallowing the hysteria she heard bubbling up in her words. "I have a brother and sister to put through college."

"Look, everybody, just relax," Lila said, "it's only a rumor, okay? There's no need for us to go off half-cocked. Everything is probably going to be fine." She glanced down at her watch. "The store's going to be opening in a half hour, Jayne," she said. "And you've got a lot of employees in here who want to make purchases. You and Amy better get on the stick if you want to open on time this morning."

"Right," Jayne said, pushing to the back of her mind for now—well, almost to the back of her mind, anyway—all thoughts of hostile takeovers. "Right," she said again, steeling herself. Work—an excessive amount of it—was exactly what she needed right now, she told herself. Something to take her mind off just how badly her morning…her week…her month had begun.

It can't possibly get any worse, she told herself again. And this time she didn't worry about jinxing herself or offending fate by doing so. Because for the first time in her life Jayne was confident that that was true. Things couldn't get any worse from here. No way. Whatever else the day ahead held, it was only going to be better.

It would be, she promised herself.

It would.

* * *

By mid-afternoon, Erik Randolph wasn't feeling quite as optimistic about his marital prospects as he had upon waking that morning. For one thing, the gloomy weather, which traditionally boded ill, anyway, had dampened his mood—so to speak. But what had dampened his mood even more was the fact that, astonishingly, of the three women to whom he had proposed marriage so far today, none had accepted his offer. None. Talk about boding ill...

The first of those women had been his sister, Celeste's, best friend, Marianne, who was enjoying a few days with Celeste at the Randolph estate before returning to graduate school. Erik had known her for years, of course, and rather liked her, even if he didn't know her all that well. Still, he had thought it reasonable that she might warm to his offer of marriage, however temporary, because Celeste had confided to him recently that Marianne had a huge crush on him.

Well, all right, so maybe Celeste's revelation hadn't been all *that* recent. Maybe it had been more than a decade ago, when Marianne was eleven, but that was beside the point. Erik had still been surprised when she declined, citing a desire to return to her studies. Her tuition for the fall semester, she had explained, had already been paid in full.

Fine, then, Erik had thought. On to prospect number two: Diana, the daughter of the Randolphs' housekeeper, Mrs. Martin. Erik had known Diana for ages, too, seeing as how Mr. and Mrs. Martin had come to work for his family when he was still in high school. But for some reason Diana hadn't seemed to think Erik was serious about his offer of marriage, had simply giggled riotously when he'd outlined his proposal, and had kept giggling no matter how hard he had insisted that he was, in fact, quite serious. Finally, wiping tears from her eyes—and still giggling—Diana had declined, thanked him, anyway, and headed off to work. He had heard her giggling all the way down the hall.

Erik's third rejection had come only moments ago, from the waitress at Crystal's on Marion Street, an upscale eatery that claimed one of Indiana's only Cordon Bleu trained chefs. And although said waitress hadn't seemed to take his suggestion quite as lightly as the other women had, she had ultimately declined due to a previous engagement—literally. She'd told Erik she felt obliged to marry her fiancé the following month.

Nevertheless, he held firm in his conviction that his search for a wife would pan out—today. He was even so sure of that, that he had dressed in his best suit, a Hugo Boss charcoal pinstripe, and a Valentino silk necktie with an elegant geometric design, knowing that such an outfit would make an impression. Now, as he approached Colette Jewelry, Erik felt more than optimistic that he was on the right track. Finding a wife with whom he could enjoy wedded bliss for a full year, he was certain, would be a piece of wedding cake.

The whimsical thought made him smile as he pushed open the door to Colette Jewelry and strode into the main showroom. He'd been in the store many times over the years, of course, to purchase baubles for his feminine companions. But where he normally turned left, toward the specialty pieces, now Erik went right, toward the wedding and engagement displays. As he strode in that direction, he overheard two women chatting, and glanced up to see that two of Colette's salesclerks were busily rearranging one of the wedding-and-engagement showcases.

Perfect, he thought. Whatever new inventory the women were putting out, that was what he wanted. He was known for being on the cutting edge of, well, just about everything. So if there was something new happening in engagement rings, Erik Randolph wanted to know about it.

The two salesclerks had their heads bowed in soft conversation, he noted as he drew nearer, presumably about the display they were in the process of putting together. So rapt was their concentration on their conversation, in fact, that they didn't even notice Erik's approach. He was about to clear his throat to make his presence known—after all, this was most uncommon at Colette, to be overlooked by the sales staff—when one of the women's remarks made him hesitate.

"I don't know what I'll do if there is a hostile takeover," said the woman closest to him, a redhead. "If Colette is gobbled up by a rival company, I could end up unemployed. Without this job, I can't possibly pay for Charlie and Chloe's tuition and living expenses."

"It's a bad situation all around," the other clerk, a brunette, agreed. "But it's just a rumor, Jayne. Don't borrow trouble."

"I can't help it, Amy," the woman identified as Jayne replied quietly, soberly. "I keep worrying about what would happen to Charlie and Chloe—and to me, too, for that matter—if I lose my job. I'm barely making ends meet as it is."

"Maybe you could go on that *Millionaire* question-and-answer show," the brunette called Amy said lightly, clearly joking. "You're pretty good with trivia. Or, better still, maybe they'll have another one of those shows about marrying a multimillionaire, and you could go on that."

"Oh, yeah," Jayne, the redheaded salesclerk, agreed with a chuckle. "Even though that one didn't *quite* turn out the way they planned," she added, "I'm sure that would solve all of *my* problems. Yeah, I'll just go out and find myself a multimillionaire to marry, if only momentarily. Because I'd probably at least wind up with some nice parting gifts, right?"

Erik snapped his mouth shut at hearing both the remark and the woman's laughter. Because the first had been a comment that was simply too serendipitous for words, and the second had been a sound that was simply too musical to ignore. Whoever the woman was, she had a wonderful laugh, one that made something pop and fizz and settle in a warm place very close to Erik's heart.

And what an interesting sensation that was, too.

When she glanced up to find Erik looking at her, he noted that she also had a charming way of blushing. Well, my, my, my. For such a gloomy day, things sure were brightening up all of a sudden.

"Hello," the redhead said softly, her voice as pleasant as her laughter had been. "Can I help you?"

Erik smiled. Oh, if she only knew.

What was it he had been thinking he required in a wife? he asked himself again as he gazed upon the redhead named Jayne. Oh, yes. First and foremost, she would have to be beautiful.

He considered the salesclerk behind the counter again, taking in the wide eyes, the fair complexion, the smattering of freckles, and the...*unusual* wardrobe that appeared to be kind of...damp?

We-ell, he thought, she *was* kind of cute. In a soggy, mismatched, ragamuffin sort of way.

"Actually, Miss..." he began, deliberately leading.

"Pembroke," she told him. Then she asked her fateful question once again. "Can I help you?"

Erik's smile fell some when he recalled that he'd also been thinking earlier that he wanted his future wife to be blond. And preferably brown-eyed, as well. He noted the pale-red hair again and thought, Fine. So she was strawberry blond. It was close enough. And although her eyes were a striking lavender color, he'd never said they absolutely *had* to be brown, had he? No, he had not. He'd simply indicated that it would be preferable, that was all. Let it never be said that Erik Randolph couldn't make compromises. Lavender eyes it would be.

"As a matter of fact, you can help me," he told her. "I'm looking for something very specific."

She smiled at him, and he decided then that he liked

her smile very much. That was going to be so helpful in the coming year.

"Well, you've come to the right place," she told him.

"Oh, I don't doubt that for a moment," he assured her, recalling that the third item on his list of wifely requirements had been reasonable intelligence and a fair amount of articulation. Even if the woman behind the counter had barely spoken two dozen words so far, she did seem to at least have the capacity for both.

Still, he had wanted the future Mrs. Randolph to be knowledgeable about current fashion trends, hadn't he? he further reminded himself. And, noting the woman's outfit once more—however reluctantly—there was no way he could make excuses for her there, could he?

Unless, of course, she was way *ahead* of Erik in fashion sense, he told himself. Which, although unlikely, was certainly possible. Who knew? Maybe a month from now, everyone who was anyone in Youngsville would be wearing burnt orange and raspberry with chartreuse accessories. Hey, it could happen. After all, bell-bottoms and fringed vests were back in style, weren't they?

He mentally tallied the rest of his wife to-do list. A demure and mild disposition had been desirable, he remembered thinking, which, clearly, this woman had. And he'd wanted his wife to be a free thinker, too. Taking in her outfit again, he realized that wasn't going to be a character trait she lacked *at all*. A knowledge of the social register—well, they could study together, he told himself—and an appreciation for the arts. Again, more studying might be required.

Ah, well. No one was perfect, he reminded himself. And they would be spending a year together, so all this studying would give them something to occupy their time. Jayne the salesclerk did, at least, seem to claim the majority of the desirable traits Erik required in a wife.

Which was good, because he decided in that moment that she was exactly the woman he needed. She had just stated quite clearly that marriage to money—temporarily, no less—would solve all of her problems. And having a woman married to his money—temporarily, no less— would solve all of Erik's problems, too. He needed a wife. She needed money. Their encounter this afternoon, clearly, was fate. It was providence. It was kismet. It was destiny.

It was perfect.

He smiled again when he realized just how well this was going to work out. Obviously, the two of them were meant for each other. Now all he had to do was convince Jayne—what was her last name again?—of that, too.

"I apologize for your having to wait," she said, just as the silence was beginning to stretch taut. "We didn't mean to ignore you. We just didn't hear you come in."

"Oh, no harm done," he assured her. "In fact, I found your conversation to be quite intriguing."

Jayne's eyes widened in obvious concern. "Ah…" she began eloquently. "You mean that, um, that stuff about a hostile takeover? Oh, that was all totally false."

"Yeah," her co-worker quickly agreed, with a very adamant nod. "That was a complete fabrication. We were just playing What-if."

Jayne nodded again. "I mean, who'd want to hostilely take over Colette, you know? It's unthinkable."

"I couldn't care less about a takeover," Erik said amiably, honestly. "Hostile or otherwise. That wasn't the part of your conversation that I found intriguing."

The two women exchanged glances, then Jayne directed her attention back to him. "Oh," she said softly.

Erik, in turn, directed his attention to the brunette. "Do you mind?" he said politely. "I think Miss…"

"Pembroke," redheaded Jayne repeated.

"Miss Pembroke, here," he continued, "can see to my needs."

The brunette gaped softly at his less-than-subtle dismissal, but she nodded and strode toward another jewelry case. Nevertheless, her watchfulness, Erik noted, didn't stray far from her colleague. Which he supposed was understandable. You never knew what kind of oddball was going to stumble in from the street and make some bizarre, unacceptable suggestion.

He turned to look again at Jayne Pembroke—*Pembroke,* he reminded himself firmly, lest he forget again; it really wouldn't do to forget one's fiancée's name, would it? *Pembroke, Pembroke, Pembroke*—calling up the most disarming smile in his ample arsenal. "No, it wasn't the takeover part of your conversation that was so intriguing," he said again. "It was the part about you marrying a multimillionaire."

Her expression, he noted, changed not one iota, save an almost imperceptible arching of one eyebrow. So he had no idea how to gauge her reaction. Very quietly she replied, "Oh." Nothing more. Just *Oh.*

So Erik plunged onward. "Because you see, I myself happen to be a multimillionaire," he told her with much equanimity.

"Oh," she said again. And again her expression reflected nothing of what she might be thinking.

Erik took it to be a good sign. Then again, he took most things, short of natural disaster, to be good signs. That was just the kind of man he was.

"Or, at least, I *will* be a multimillionaire," he clarified pleasantly. "Once I get married, I mean."

Jayne Pembroke's expression cleared then, making her look...relieved? Maybe this was going to be easier than he'd anticipated.

"So you've come in to buy an engagement ring for your intended," she said, her smile returning.

"Yes," he agreed happily. "That's it exactly. A ring. A fiancée—and, hence, a wife—will, after all, expect a ring, won't she? Two rings, actually. One to signify the engagement and one to signify the marriage. Which," he added, "when you get right down to it, is a damned nice gift, considering the fact that she will only be my wife for one year.''

Now Jayne's smile fell again, and her expression grew puzzled. ''One year?'' she echoed, sounding disappointed.

''Well, you can't expect me to stay married any longer than is necessary, can you?'' Erik asked, fighting a twinge of indignation. Honestly. They weren't even married yet, and already she was finding fault with him. ''I mean, I do have other obligations, you know.''

Now Jayne opened her mouth to speak, but no words emerged.

''Not that my wife will have to worry,'' he said, jacking up the wattage on his smile. ''Because it goes without saying that, after we go our separate ways, she will end up with some—'' he wiggled his eyebrows meaningfully ''—lovely parting gifts.''

Now Jayne, he noted, was looking at him as if she had just discovered he'd escaped from a hospital for the criminally insane. Hmmm, he thought. Perhaps they weren't quite on the same wavelength as he had assumed they were. Perhaps he wasn't going about this the best way he could be going about it. Perhaps he wasn't making himself as clear as he could be making himself.

So Erik straightened to his full six feet, tossed his head in a way that he'd been told by several women was quite boyish and charming, brushed his dark hair back from his forehead, and smiled what he liked to think was his rogue's smile. ''What I'm trying to say, Miss Pembroke,'' he began in his most enchanting tone of voice, ''is…will you marry me?''

Three
─────

Jayne eyed the man standing on the other side of the counter very cautiously, and debated for a full fifteen seconds whether or not she should stomp her foot down—hard—on the alarm button located conveniently behind the jewelry showcase. He didn't *look* like a psychotic, crazed, homicidal maniac. In fact, she thought upon further consideration of his charmingly disheveled dark hair and kind, bittersweet-chocolate brown eyes, he was actually kind of cute. But one could never tell these days. Ultimately, being the kind of woman that she was, she decided to give him the benefit of the doubt.

And also, being the kind of woman that she was, she decided to speak slowly and not make any sudden moves.

"Uuummm," she began, stringing the single syllable out over several time zones. "That's uh..." She cleared her throat indelicately and tried again. "That's really nice of you to ask, Mr. um..."

The potentially psychotic, crazed, homicidal—but kind

of cute—maniac closed his eyes in what appeared to be genuine embarrassment, pressed his fingertips lightly against his forehead, made a soft tsking sound and looked very sheepish.

"I'm sorry," he said. "I haven't even introduced myself, have I? I can't imagine what you must be thinking of me, proposing this way when I haven't even told you who I am." He opened his eyes again and extended his hand toward her. "Erik Randolph," he said by way of an introduction.

Oh, well, that explained everything, Jayne thought as relief coursed through her. Even though she had only moved into 20 Amber Court a month ago, she had grown up in Youngsville, so she knew all about the Randolph family. They were like local royalty. They kept the society pages of the *Youngsville Gazette* in business. The Randolphs were purported to be one of the wealthiest families in the state of Indiana. And they were rumored to be one of the most eccentric families in the state, too, from what Jayne had heard and read.

If Erik, here, was any indication, the eccentricity thing was no rumor at all.

Still, from all accounts the Randolphs were harmless. They were, in fact, gregarious, magnanimous people, known throughout several states for their wealth, their prominence, their numerous and varied social causes and their limitless philanthropy. But never had she heard anyone refer to any of the Randolphs as psychotic, crazed *or* homicidal. Which, naturally, was quite a relief.

Nevertheless, she still felt a bit cautious as she extended her own hand and shook his. Then he grinned as he gripped her fingers firmly—but not homicidally or maniacally—and Jayne relaxed.

"Mr. Randolph," she said, feeling glad that she had hesitated setting off the alarm. "It's lovely to meet you," she added, uncertain what else to say. After all, she couldn't very well tell him she accepted his proposal, could she? As an afterthought she added, "I've heard so much about you."

He nodded amiably, as if he was in no way surprised to hear her say this. "All good things, I hope."

"Oh, yes," she assured him. "From all reports, you're quite the charmer." *And also quite the odd duck,* she added to herself.

"Well then, you have me at a disadvantage," he told her, still smiling, still relaxing her. "Because I'm afraid I know little about you. Other than the fact that you, too, appear to be quite charming. And that you are in need of a wealthy husband. Which," he hurried on before she had a chance to contradict him, "works out perfectly, because I, in addition to being wealthy, am in need of a wife."

Oh, dear, Jayne thought. They were back to that, were they? Very diplomatically she said, "Well, I wish you luck in your search, and I'll be happy to assist you in finding the perfect ring to present to your fiancée. But I couldn't possibly accept your offer myself." She smiled, too, what she hoped was a kind—and in no way homicidal-mania-provoking, just in case—smile. "Even if I know *of* you, I don't *know* you. So I really couldn't accept your proposal. Not that I'm not flattered," she hastened to add for good measure. "Now about that ring," she hurried on further. "Personally, I think the square-cut diamonds are just so lovely, especially in the white-gold setting, and very—"

But Erik Randolph was not to be dissuaded that easily. "No, no, no," he interrupted her gently. "You don't understand. It isn't necessary for my wife to know me."

Jayne arched her brows curiously. *Eccentric,* she thought, really wasn't an accurate word for Erik Randolph. No, she was beginning to think the term *delusional* might better describe him. "Oh?" she said.

He nodded knowingly. "The marriage will be in name only," he told her. "Oh, certainly, we'll have to live to-

gether, to fulfill the terms of the agreement, but that won't
be a problem.''

Wondering what it was that made her prolong this discussion, Jayne nevertheless asked, ''Um, no?''

''Certainly not.''

Well, naturally, a *man* would think that way, she
thought. Especially a delusional—oops, she meant *eccentric,* of course—man like Erik Randolph. But Jayne kept
the observation to herself and, in an effort to conclude
this part of their dialogue and move on to the next, said
instead, ''Well, I'm sure you'll find the right woman soon.
Now then, we have a very good selection of square-cut
solitaires that you might find—''

Before she had a chance to direct his attention to the
jewelry showcase, however, Erik interrupted her again.
''Oh, I believe I've already found the right woman,'' he
said.

Oh, Jayne didn't *think* so. She met his gaze again—
really, he did have the most beautiful brown eyes, thickly
lashed and so dark she could scarcely see where the irises
ended and the pupils began and…and…and…

And what was it they had been talking about? she wondered vaguely. Oh, yes. He had asked her to marry him,
and she was trying to explain why she couldn't.

It was all coming back to her now.

''Yes, well, as I said,'' she tried again, ''I'm very flattered that you would ask, Mr. Randolph, but I really can't
marry you. Truly, I can't. I'm afraid I decided a long time
ago that before I married a man, I wanted to, well, know
him. And being in love with him would be even more
helpful. But thank you, anyway. Now about that ring for
your intended, whoever she might turn out to be…''

Jayne tried once more to turn his attention to the array
of sparkling diamond rings that lay in the glass case between them. But Erik Randolph would have none of it.
Instead of focusing his attention on the exquisite gems,
he eyed Jayne with much consideration and interest.

"You don't think I'm serious, do you?" he asked.

Actually, Jayne suspected he *was* serious. Which was entirely the problem. Aloud, however, she only said, "Well, can you blame me?"

"I suppose it does make sense that you would draw such a conclusion," he conceded. "How often do strangers come in from the street and propose marriage, right?"

"I think I can safely say that you're my first."

For some reason, he smiled *very* suggestively at that. Then, "Well, I assure you, Jayne Pembroke, that I am completely serious. I want you to marry me."

"You fell in love with me at first sight, is that it?" she asked playfully.

"Don't be silly," he countered. "I don't even know you."

"Oh."

"Besides, I don't believe in love at first sight. Or any sight, for that matter." Before Jayne could comment on that—not that she had any idea what to say—he continued, "As I said, the marriage I'm proposing would be in name only. A marriage of convenience, if you will. I'll be turning thirty soon. And my grandfather, a lovable old rogue, I assure you, decided a long time ago that I should be married by the time I turn thirty. In fact, he's blackmailing me into it."

"Can't you talk to him? Explain that you don't want to get married?"

"No," Erik said. "I can't."

"Why not?"

"He's dead, you see."

"Oh. I'm sorry."

Erik Randolph looked genuinely bereft as he said, "I am, too. But he was a lovable old rogue, as I said, and I do believe he only wanted what he thought was best for me."

"And what did he think was best for you?"

"The love of a good woman," Erik replied promptly.

"Oh," Jayne said, smiling in spite of the strange situation. "Oh, that's so sweet."

"And also one-third of his $180 million-dollar estate," Erik added, in as matter-of-fact a tone as Jayne had ever heard.

Then his words hit her, and her mouth dropped open slightly, an incredulous little gasp of air escaping. "One-third of…of…of…"

"Sixty million dollars is what it boils down to." Erik did the math for her, in that same matter-of-fact tone, by golly, when Jayne wasn't quite able to calculate—or enunciate—the amount herself.

"Well," she finally got out. "Well. Well, gee. Well, that's pretty doggone good," she conceded with much understatement.

Erik nodded, apparently oblivious to her complete astonishment, as if everyone came into $60 million because their lovable rogue of a grandfather willed it to them. "Unfortunately," he said, "Grandfather Randolph insisted on one small stipulation before I could inherit. That I be married. By the time I'm thirty."

"And you'll be thirty soon," Jayne echoed his earlier sentiment.

He nodded again. "Very soon. In two weeks, to be precise."

This time Jayne's jaw dropped a lot more, and the gasp of incredulous breath that escaped was more like a great big whoosh of air. *"Two weeks?"* she repeated.

He nodded once more.

"You expect to find a woman who'll marry you in two weeks' time?"

He eyed her with much concern. "Do you think that's unreasonable?"

Jayne couldn't believe what she was hearing. He honestly seemed to think he could just waltz right in off the street and ask a woman to marry him, just because he would be coming into $60 million as a result. Then again, she thought, there were probably lots of women out there who would do just that. Especially once they got a look at Erik Randolph in his expertly tailored dark suit, with his silky, dark-brown hair and puppy dog brown eyes and full mouth that was just made for kissing and—

Well, suffice it to say that there were probably plenty of women who would take him up on his offer. Women other than Jayne Pembroke, anyway.

"Um, look," she said, striving for a polite way to tell him he was nuts. "I'm really flattered," she said again, "and I wish you well in your search, and I hope you enjoy your…" she swallowed with some difficulty before finally getting out "—$60 million. But I'm not the woman you need, truly."

He eyed her intently for a moment, saying nothing. Then he asked, "Would you at least let me take you to dinner tonight?"

Jayne shook her head. But she was surprised at how reluctant she felt when she told him, "No, I'm afraid not. Thank you."

"Oh, please," he said. "I can explain things better, and you might change your mind. Plus, it would give you *hours* to get to know me."

She couldn't quite prevent the smile that curled her lips in response to both his cajoling and his own earnest grin. "No, really," she told him. But she could feel her conviction slipping, and she was certain that Erik detected it, too, because his smile grew broader still.

"And once you get to know me," he added, "you'll discover just how charming and irresistible—not to mention what a great catch—I am."

Jayne had no idea why, but she found herself wanting to say yes to his offer. Not the marriage offer, of course—that would be silly—but the dinner offer. Had he been another man who had wandered in off the street and flirted with her, one who *wasn't* rumored to be eccentric, and one who *hadn't* just proposed marriage to a total stranger, she might very well have given his invitation serious consideration. He *was* kind of charming and irresistible, after all. Not to mention cute. And he was seeming less and less like a psychotic, crazed homicidal maniac with every passing moment.

So that was a definite plus.

"I'm not sure it would be a good idea," she said halfheartedly. She told herself she was trying to let him down easily. But she knew she was really only stalling for time, because she discovered then that—surprise, surprise—she really wanted to accept his invitation.

Erik, however, still clearly picking up on her uncertainty, pressed, "Look, if you're worried about my intentions, you don't have to tell me where you live. You can meet me somewhere."

"Gee, I don't know…"

"And I'll let you pick the restaurant."

"But…"

"And choose the time."

"It's just that…"

"Please, Jayne," he said. "You may well be my only hope. And once I explain the situation to you, you might change your mind."

She wasn't sure how she should take that first part of his statement, whether being his only hope was a good thing or a bad thing. But she was absolutely certain about the last part of his statement—there was no way she would change her mind, no matter how well she understood what he termed "the situation."

Still, what would it hurt to have dinner with him? she thought. It wasn't as though she planned to do anything else this evening. Oh, wait a minute. Yes, she did have plans, she suddenly remembered. She planned to do laundry.

Dinner with Erik was definitely looking better now.

"It will all make sense to you when I explain," he promised, swaying her further.

Jayne gazed into his eyes, nearly losing herself in their dark-brown depths. He was allowing her to call all the shots, letting her set up their date—or whatever it was—in any way that would make her feel safe and comfortable. Just because he had a reputation for being eccentric, that was no reason to say no, was it? she asked herself. Were he any other charming, irresistible and cute—did she mention cute?—man asking her out to dinner under the same circumstances, she'd probably say yes.

And he was *awfully* cute.

"Look, I'll tell you what," Erik said when she still didn't reply one way or the other to his invitation. "J.J.'s Deli is right up the street. What time do you get off from work?"

"Five," Jayne said before she could stop herself.

He smiled. "Fine. I'll be at J.J.'s Deli at seven o'clock tonight. If you decide to come, wonderful. If you decide not to…"

His voice trailed off, and she was surprised at the depth of disappointment she heard in it.

"If you decide not to," he said again, sighing heavily, "well, I guess I'll survive. Somehow."

She smiled back at him, but still couldn't quite bring herself to accept.

"But I think, Jayne, that if you do decide to come, we could have a very nice time, and a very interesting conversation. Seven o'clock," he repeated. "J.J.'s Deli. I hope you'll come."

And then Erik Randolph, eccentric, cute guy, potential multimillionaire, spun around and exited Colette without a backward glance.

And all Jayne could do was shake her head in mystification, and wonder what on earth had just happened.

Shortly after arriving home at five-thirty that evening—stumbling over Mojo as she did, because the blasted cat was, as usual, lying in wait for her, to trip her as she came through the front door—Jayne noted the flashing light on her answering machine indicating that she had received two calls. And she immediately sensed that her terrible, no-good, very bad day wasn't over quite yet. And, too, she wondered when she would learn not to jinx herself by being so bloody optimistic all the time.

The first message assured her that she was right, and it prevented her from playing the second message until she got the first straightened out. Because that first message, although short and simple—"Jayne, call me because there's something we need to discuss"—definitely had an ominous ring to it. A good reason for that might have been because the message came from her financial advisor.

What felt like hours later but must only have been a matter of minutes, Jayne hung up the phone again, having discovered that one of the "sure thing" investments of which she had been encouraged to take advantage hadn't been such a sure thing, after all, but that she shouldn't worry, because she hadn't lost *that* much money, really, and she *would* recover her loss, eventually, and that recovery would be possible in a very short time, say one or two years—three at the most—but in the meantime, her finances weren't going to be quite as fluid as they had been, so that might be a problem for a little while.

Jayne had had to laugh—albeit with a touch of hysteria—at that part about her finances not being quite as fluid as they had been, because they were barely a trickle as it was. Just what, she had asked her advisor, did "not quite as fluid" mean? Wherein he offered her a very detailed explanation that amounted, pretty much, to the fact that she wouldn't have enough money to pay any more college tuition for her brother and sister until the year 2003—2004 at the latest.

This, Jayne decided immediately, was going to present something of a problem. The current semester was cov-

ered, because she had paid that bill a month ago. Come
spring, however…

Oh, dear. She really had been planning to give her
brother and sister something for Christmas other than *the
shaft.*

How was she going to tell Chloe and Charlie that they
wouldn't be able to attend college after this, their first
semester? She could still remember the joy sparkling in
her siblings' eyes when they'd all said their goodbyes at
Indiana University scarcely a week ago. The twins had
been so excited about starting their studies, and over pizza
and later brownies, the three of them had made such plans
for the future. Jayne would do almost anything to preserve
those plans, that excitement, that joy.

Almost anything.

She sighed heavily, gazing longingly at the telephone,
wondering how on earth she was going to fix things this
time. Because Jayne fully intended to fix things. She
didn't know how yet, but she would figure out something.
She wasn't about to tell Chloe and Charlie they'd have to
quit school. She *would* fix things.

Because that was what Jayne did.

For the last four years, that was what she had been.
Jayne the fixer. Since her parents' deaths, she had done
whatever she could to ease the twins' grief along with her
own. She had been there for the two of them no matter
what. Whenever one or both of them had needed her, for
whatever reason, Jayne had dropped what she was doing
and remedied the situation, however she could.

Usually those remedies had consisted of a bandage on
a sprain or help with homework or stretching a pound of
hamburger into three separate meals. Whatever the problem had been, Jayne had somehow found a way to fix it.
This time, though…

She sighed again. There was no quick fix for the loss
of a large sum of money. Not unless one won the lottery,
and Jayne—call her crazy—simply wasn't willing to put

her faith in that. Not unless one happened to stumble upon another large sum of money somewhere to replace the loss. Not unless one stumbled upon some*one* who had a large sum of money to replace it.

Because you see, I myself happen to be a multimillionaire. Or, at least, I will *be a multimillionaire. Once I get married.*

Oh, dear, Jayne thought. That was the last thing—the last voice—she needed to be hearing in her head right now. Accepting Erik Randolph's proposal was *not* going to be the fix for this particular problem.

The marriage will be in name only.

That didn't matter, she told herself. There were all kinds of things that could go wrong in an arrangement like that. She wanted no part of it. Yes, she would do almost anything to keep her siblings in college. The operative word in that avowal, however, was *almost*. There was no way Jayne would marry a complete stranger just to keep her siblings in school.

Though she supposed she could argue he wasn't a *complete* stranger. She did know him by reputation. And they had enjoyed a nice, if superficial—and borderline surreal—conversation that afternoon. There were still a host of reasons why she couldn't—wouldn't—marry Erik Randolph.

Oh, certainly, we'll have to live together, to fulfill the terms of the agreement, but that won't be a problem.

And that was just the first of those hosts of reasons.

The arrangement will only last one year.

That was beside the point. The point was—

The flashing red light on the phone caught Jayne's attention again, and she was grateful for the interruption into her mental argument with Erik Randolph. Honestly, she thought, they weren't even married yet, and already they were disagreeing about things.

Not that she had any intention of marrying him, she

hastily reminded herself. It was just a hypothetical argument, that was all.

Oh, bother, she thought, pinching the bridge of her nose to ward off a headache that came out of nowhere. *Just play the next message, Jayne. Maybe it will be good news.*

She realized it was indeed good news the moment she heard the sound of her sister's voice. There was nothing Jayne liked more than hearing Chloe and Charlie's reports from the collegiate front, which had come pretty much daily since the beginning of the semester.

"Hi, Jaynie!" Chloe's voice chirped from the answering machine. In the background, Jayne could hear Charlie's voice, as well, a shout of "Hey, big sister, whassup?" and she smiled.

"Hello, Chloe. Hello, Charlie," she said, even though she knew they couldn't hear her.

"We just called to say hi and to tell you that we wrote a poem for you today in our Intro to Creative Writing class."

This announcement was followed by Chloe's clearing of her throat, Charlie's mimicking of an opera star warming up with a deep, resonant "Mi-mi-mi" and Jayne's laughter at both. Then her brother and sister began, in unison, to read their composition.

"*J* is for Jaynie, our sister so fair, *A* is for altruistic, unlike a bear." This was punctuated with giggling, and Charlie's murmuring of "I told you that line needed work." Then the twins began again, more soberly this time. "*Y* is for youth, which she gave up too soon. *N* is for niceness, by far her greatest boon. And *E* is for everything that she does for us, and also for everything she's given up for us.

"Okay, so the rhythm's off a little bit here and there, especially at the end," Chloe said hastily. "And the last rhyme wasn't so hot, either. It's our first poem, and we wanted to write it for you." There was a small pause, then Chloe and Charlie together said, "We love you, Jaynie." Charlie added, "And we just want you to know how much we appreciate everything you've done for us. Everything is great here."

"We *love* it at IU," Chloe added. "Call when you can. Kiss Mojo for me. We'll talk to you soon."

And then the soft buzz of the dial tone filled the air for a moment before going silent.

Only then did Jayne realize there were tears in her eyes. And not because she feared her brother and sister were going to flunk creative writing, either. But because she knew in that moment that she really would do anything to make sure they stayed in school.

Even if it meant marrying an eccentric—but cute—guy like Erik Randolph.

The least she could do, she told herself, was meet him for dinner as they had arranged, and listen to what he had to say. Maybe he wasn't as crazy as he sounded. Maybe what he was proposing would be the perfect arrangement for both of them. Maybe her encounter with him this morning was simple fate and everything would work out for the best.

And maybe, Jayne thought further, while she was sleeping tonight, the blue fairy would fly into her bedroom and turn her into a real boy.

Resigned to at least hear Erik Randolph out—and recalling that all of her matching clothes were in the laundry—Jayne picked up the phone again. This time it was to call her upstairs neighbor Lila, to see if she could borrow that cute little yellow dress the other woman had worn to the company picnic last month....

Four

She isn't coming.

The thought circled through Erik's head for the umpteenth time as he rearranged the salt and pepper shakers on the table before him for the umpteenth time. And even though Jayne hadn't actually promised to meet him at the restaurant, he was surprised by the realization that she wasn't going to show. Somehow he had been so sure that she would come tonight. She had seemed like she wanted to accept his invitation, even if she hadn't quite.

But it was now twenty past the hour, and Erik couldn't conceive of anything that would make someone run that late for an engagement—he smiled at his unintentional double entendre in spite of his gloomy mood—unless it was that the someone in question simply wasn't coming.

She isn't coming, he thought again. And his realization of that caused him to feel surprisingly melancholy.

Oh, sure, he knew that what he'd proposed to Jayne Pembroke earlier that day was unconventional, to say the least. She had been understandably wary. But by the time they'd parted ways, she had seemed amenable to at least meeting him tonight and hearing him out. And although he sympathized fairly well with what it must be like to be a woman in contemporary American society, where too many men were, well, pigs, Erik liked to think that he, at least, exuded an aura of allure and reputation that raised him well above the sty.

Still, he conceded, it probably wasn't every day that a woman was proposed to by a complete stranger. Even one as charming and irresistible as he. Especially dressed as he was in another of his best suits, this one a Brioni the color of bittersweet chocolate, to enhance what he cheerfully considered to be his dark, brooding good looks. Despite that...

She isn't coming.

He was surprised by the depth of his disappointment. He told himself his distress simply stemmed from the fact that he would now have to go back to square one in his hunt for a wife. But deep down he suspected his distress might well be the result of something else entirely. What that something else might be, though, he was reluctant to ponder. He only knew that at the moment he was unhappy, and that unhappiness had come about because he wouldn't be seeing Jayne tonight.

And that was a very odd development. Because it wasn't easy to make Erik Randolph unhappy, especially when it came to women. He had a naturally optimistic nature, a generally positive outlook on life, and it just took a lot to get him down. Women, in particular, had never seemed to him to be the kind of thing to lose any sleep over. Even the ones he found himself serious enough about to date for an extended period of time—like two months or so. Erik simply never got worked up enough over a member of the opposite sex to feel unhappy when that member wasn't around. But having had just one brief conversation with Jayne Pembroke that afternoon, he still found himself missing her this evening.

It was more than a little peculiar.

He sighed heavily and was about to stand—what was the point of staying?—when a flash of pale yellow near the entrance caught his attention. Erik turned his gaze hopefully in that direction, his heart rate accelerating to a rapid pace. But his hope was short-lived—and his heart rate slowed down again—when he saw that the woman who entered the delicatessen wasn't the one he had been expecting.

At least, he thought further, as a sliver of doubt wedged itself into his brain, he didn't *think* that was Jayne Pembroke....

The woman said something to the hostess, who nodded and said something back, then pointed in Erik's direction. And when the woman in pale yellow turned toward him, his heart nearly stopped beating entirely. Because it *was* Jayne Pembroke, he realized. And she *wasn't* the woman he'd been expecting.

And *boy,* was he glad he'd waited for her.

She grinned shyly when she saw him, then began to make her way toward the table he had chosen—one situated in the far rear corner, where, he had thought, they might have some degree of privacy. J.J.'s Deli was a basic delicatessen, small in scope, but with a high, bare-beamed ceiling, terra-cotta tiled floors and brick walls decorated with bright poster art of old movies. The front served carry-out clientele, but a handful of tables was scattered along the back for those who wanted to take their time as they ate. During the day, the place was usually packed, inside and out, situated as it was in the heart of Youngsville business district. At nearly seven-thirty on a Monday night, however, the place was fairly deserted.

As he watched Jayne approach, Erik told himself she shouldn't look out of place there, dressed in her simple, casual, yellow dress, with a pale-blue sweater tossed over her shoulders. But somehow he got the impression of European royalty as she drew nearer.

Had he been worrying about the impression he would make? he asked himself. Because if he was making an impression on her that was half as good as the one she was making on him, then he ought to be—speaking of old movies—in like Flynn.

"Hi," she said softly, when she came to a stop in front of him.

Her hair, which had been tersely bound that afternoon, was now piled loosely atop her head, held in place by some invisible means of support, with a few errant tendrils spiraling down around her face. Her violet eyes seemed even more violet than they had been that afternoon, and he was even more enchanted by the light dusting of freckles that dotted the bridge of her nose and her cheekbones. The only makeup he could detect was a soft pink applied to her lips, a color mirrored by the pale lacquer on the fingers that clutched a tiny, pale-blue satin purse in front of her.

Her most intriguing accessory, though, was a pin affixed to her sweater, an unusual but very lovely brooch that picked up on the color of her dress. Amber, he guessed, his knowledge of jewelry surprisingly good for a layman. But he couldn't quite place the designer or origin of the piece. Still, it was quite exquisite.

Okay, so maybe the fashion thing wasn't going to be a problem after all, Erik thought. Because at the moment she looked as if she had just stepped off the cover of a magazine, one devoted to ultrafemininity. Somewhere deep inside him, in a place he hadn't known existed, his testosterone levels fairly shot through the roof.

All in all, it was not an unpleasant sensation.

She was nervous, he noted, and the realization relieved him. Because it meant that the two of them were meeting on equal ground.

"Hi," he greeted her back. But he was damned if he could think of a single other thing to say.

Some latent sense of courtesy made him rise from his chair and move to the one beside it. He pulled it out for her, and she smiled before seating herself, another point in her favor. Erik was a firm believer in equality for both sexes, but it bugged the hell out of him whenever a woman rejected a perfectly good offer of common courtesy, citing the women's movement for her refusal.

When he seated himself again, he caught the waiter's attention and silently bid him come over. Then he ordered two glasses of pinot griggio and the focaccia bread and brie appetizer, and sent the man on his way.

"I was afraid you weren't coming," he told Jayne the moment their server was out of earshot.

"I'm sorry I'm late," she apologized. "I—" She stopped suddenly, as if whatever she'd intended to tell him had fled her brain completely. Then she shrugged philosophically. "I'm afraid it's been one of those days," she finally said.

Erik propped his elbow on the table, cupped his chin in his hand and eyed her with much appreciation. "Hasn't it just?" he agreed with a smile.

She smiled back, another one of those soft, shy smiles that set his heart to humming happily in his chest. Oh, yes. He was definitely glad he had waited for her. And he very much looked forward to whatever other surprises the evening held.

Somewhere at the back of his muddled brain, Erik realized that the conversation had stalled immediately after the sharing of greetings, something which made him a truly dreadful example of a host. With a swift, mental kick to his chat center, he straightened, wove his fingers together on the tabletop and tried again.

"So. Jayne. How long have you worked for Colette? I don't recall seeing you in the store before today."

"Oh, are you a regular customer at Colette?" she asked, her interest quite, *quite* piqued.

Hmm, Erik thought, backpedaling. It might not be a good idea to start off his wooing of a prospective wife—however temporary she might be—by telling her how often he was in her place of employment to buy gifts for other women of his acquaintance. "I, ah… I've been in a time or two recently. With my sister," he hastened to clarify. "Or my mother." He angled his wrist toward her as he added, "And not long ago I had my watch repaired there."

She nodded. She also seemed to be relieved by the benign choice of subject matter, because she continued to smile as she replied, "I've only worked there for about a month. But I've lived in Youngsville all my life. In fact, I moved into my own apartment just recently."

Erik's own curiosity now was quite piqued. "Why the move?" he asked. "Finally getting out from under your parents' thumbs?"

And why did the prospect of doing such a thing sound so appealing to him all of a sudden?

She shook her head. "No, my parents passed away when I was eighteen."

Oh, well done, Erik, he thought morosely. Nothing like bringing up a sad subject to set their conversation off on the right foot. "I'm sorry," he said.

She nodded. "Me, too," she told him. "But it's been four years. I'm coping." With one small sigh, she continued, "But my brother and sister, who I've been raising since my parents' deaths, headed off to IU this year—they're twins—so I'm on my own now, and I thought it was time for a change."

"And do you like having your own place?" Erik asked idly, trying to steer the conversation back into safe—ergo, not sad—waters.

"Oh, I love it," she replied enthusiastically. "But I do miss Chloe and Charlie."

"Well, I, for one, am glad you decided to stay here in town, instead of following them off to Bloomington."

That shy smile again—which really was so enchanting—then, "Thank you," she said. "I'm glad, too. Besides, Bloomington isn't so far away that I can't see them fairly regularly."

They eased into a comfortable chitchat mode for the next fifteen or twenty minutes, pausing only when their server returned with their wine and appetizer and to take their orders for dinner. Then it was right back into the small talk again, an activity that Erik found oddly enjoyable. Normally he wasn't the biggest fan of small talk, and viewed it simply as a means to an end—that end generally being an invitation into the woman's bed, or vice versa.

Tonight, though, small talk was taking on a whole new meaning. It was still a means to an end, to be sure, but suddenly that end wasn't so much being invited into Jayne Pembroke's bed as it was…getting to know her better. Not that Erik would turn down such an invitation, should she extend it, but that wasn't the primary reason for this exchange of information. Nor, he was sure, would such an invitation be forthcoming. Not yet, anyway. No, this exchange, he realized, was coming about because he genuinely wanted to know more about her as a person.

What a concept.

And my, but the big things he discovered about Jayne Pembroke as they talked small. He learned, for example, more about the struggles she had overcome while caring for her two younger siblings. Erik couldn't imagine taking on the responsibility for someone else—*two* someone elses—like that, especially at such a young age. Jayne, however, had done so without a second thought. She'd even postponed her own college education until her brother and sister completed theirs.

It was that last tidbit of information that Erik found most amenable to his needs. "And how have you been paying for all this, Jayne?'' he asked as he watched her stir cream into her coffee after the last remnants of their dinner had been cleared away. "It must be expensive, sending two people to school, while maintaining an acceptable living standard for oneself. How do you manage it, on your paychecks from Colette?''

She stumbled in her motions when he posed the question, her hand nearly flicking the spoon right out of her mug. "Well, I, um, I, ah… That is to say…'' She sighed fitfully and avoided his gaze most steadfastly. "Well, I *do* make a nice commission,'' she finally told him.

"Oh, I don't doubt that you're a very good salesclerk,'' he conceded. "But unless you're planning to unload the crown jewels on someone…''

She indulged in a bit more avoiding of his gaze, then, "Actually,'' she said, "until recently, everything was fine.''

Hmmm, Erik thought. This could be significant. "How recently?'' he asked.

She continued to avoid his gaze as she said, "Oh, until this afternoon.''

Oh, yes, he thought. This could be *very* significant. "Before or after we spoke at the store?'' he asked.

"Um, after.''

Aha, he thought. Aloud, however, he only said, "Ah.''

"I mean, I thought we were financially sound,'' she finally told him. "I thought I had invested my parents' assets and life insurance settlement very well.''

"You *thought?*'' Erik echoed. "As in past tense?''

She removed her spoon from her mug and lifted the latter to her mouth for a sip, and still avoided his gaze most steadfastly. Erik thought her evasion highly significant indeed. And not a little encouraging.

"Yes, well, I kind of got some bad news today,'' she said.

Well, this was good news, Erik thought. "Oh?'' he asked.

She sipped her coffee experimentally, seemed to savor the flavor for a moment, replaced her cup on the table…and continued avoiding his gaze.

Yes, he thought, very good news.

"Yes," she said, "very bad news. It seems some of those investments I thought were so sound weren't quite as sound as I thought they were."

"No?"

She shook her head. "And now paying for Charlie and Chloe's tuition is going to be something of a hardship for me. In fact, it's going to be an impossibility."

Erik eyed her thoughtfully for a moment. So this was why she had come to meet him, after all, he thought. His proposal of a marriage of convenience seemed more convenient now to her than it had earlier. Perhaps fate really had stepped in, he thought. He'd already considered his meeting up with Jayne this afternoon to be serendipitous. Perhaps she was beginning to see things the same way herself.

"Well," he began, placing his own coffee mug on the table. He folded one hand atop the other and eyed her pointedly, silently willing her to look up and meet his gaze. After a brief moment of fighting it, she finally did. "Perhaps," he began again, "I can make that hardship much easier for you. Perhaps I can make that impossibility very possible indeed. And you, in turn," he added, "can help me out, as well."

"I'm not saying I'll marry you," she hastened to clarify.

"Aren't you?" he asked.

She shook her head slowly. "Only that I'll listen to what you have to say."

"Fair enough," he told her, confident that once he had outlined his plan, she would readily agree to the terms. Especially now that he knew her weakness—the twin siblings for whom she had been caring, for the past four years. They would be Erik's ace in the hole. First, though, he had to convince her that she needed him as much as he needed her.

"Well then, Jayne," he said with a smile. "Let me tell you exactly what I...propose."

Jayne listened to Erik's proposal as he outlined it, telling herself she was doing so with an *open* mind and not a *lost* one. Even so, a lost mind went a lot further toward explaining her desire to accept his offer than an open mind did. Because that was exactly what Jayne found herself wanting to do as she absorbed everything Erik told her. Accept his proposal. Marry him. Live with him—in name only—under one roof for a full year. And in exchange, take advantage of his fortune and allow him to pay for Chloe and Charlie's college expenses.

Because that was what he offered to do—take care of any costs incurred by sending two people to college for four years. Five or six years, if either—or both—of her siblings decided to go for their master's degrees. It was a very generous offer, she had to admit. Though, granted, with sixty million dollars in his wallet, the expense would be negligible to Erik. Nevertheless, it was the kind of offer a woman like Jayne would find very difficult to refuse.

And he would, of course, he promised, put it all in writing, in the form of a prenuptial agreement. He also offered what he termed "a substantial settlement" to Jayne, as well, once they dissolved their marriage, but she had declined that. Marrying for money seemed less tawdry somehow when she was doing it for someone else instead of herself. As long as she didn't benefit personally from the arrangement, then it didn't make her a gold-digger, did it?

Oh, way to justify, Jayne.

Besides, where was the harm in marrying Erik for a year? she asked herself. The relationship would be totally platonic. They'd share a roof, but nothing more. They'd have two separate rooms, two separate schedules, two separate lives. She wouldn't even have to change her name, she thought. Which, of course, she wouldn't, because what was the point when she'd just be changing it back in twelve months' time?

"If I do this," she said cautiously when he was finished describing his plan, "and I'm not saying I will," she hastened to add when she saw him smile, "there's one requirement I ask of you."

"Anything," he told her.

She hesitated only a moment before telling him, "I don't want Chloe and Charlie to know that I married you for your money."

He gazed at her thoughtfully for a moment. "Fine," he said. "Do you mind if I ask why?"

"I just don't want them to know the reason," she said, not sure she could fully explain her desire.

Maybe it was because she didn't want Chloe and Charlie to worry about her. Or maybe it was because she didn't want to tarnish their opinion of her. Maybe it was just because, as had been the case for four years, she wanted to protect them from those aspects of life that were less than stellar. And she didn't want them to know their financial difficulties were bad enough to warrant her doing something this desperate. Most of all, she didn't want them to think badly of her for doing it.

"I want Chloe and Charlie to think the reason we married is because we're in love."

Erik continued to study her in thoughtful silence for a moment, then, "Don't you think that will make it more difficult to explain things to them a year from now, when we file for divorce?" he asked.

"I have a year between now and then to think about that," Jayne said. "It won't be that bad. We can arrange it that you have little contact with them, so they won't end up liking you and missing you when you're gone."

"Oh?" Erik asked lightly. "Why, Jayne, you're hurting my feelings. I like to think I'm unforgettable."

She smiled. Oh, she was confident that was true. Something told her that fifty years from now, she'd still be looking back on her memories of Erik Randolph quite fondly. "If something comes up, and Chloe and Charlie come home for a visit, we'll just arrange for you to be traveling overseas or something."

"Fine," he conceded. "Fair enough."

"And just to be sure that Charlie and Chloe don't find out," Jayne added, realizing she sounded as if she'd already made a decision here, "my friends at 20 Amber Court have to think we're marrying for love, too. I don't want to risk anyone slipping up and saying something in front of the twins."

There was more thoughtful silence from Erik for a moment, then he asked, "And just what would we have to do to convince everyone we married out of love, instead of convenience?"

Oh, she really wished he hadn't asked that. Now Jayne was the one to eye him in thoughtful silence, as she considered her response.

Finally, she shrugged lightly and told him, "When we're around other people, we'll have to do the usual things that lovers do. Hold hands. Smile engagingly at each other. Address each other by terms of endearment. That sort of thing."

"That doesn't sound so bad," Erik said. "I can do that. And trust me. I can be *very* convincing."

Hmmm, Jayne thought. She wasn't sure if she should be worried about that or not.

"However," he added, "I won't call you Snookums, so you can put that right out of your head this very minute."

She chuckled. "Frankly, that suits me just as well. Calling me 'My darling, dearest, most perfect wife' will do just fine."

Then another concern wedged its way into her head. "You said we'll have to live together. Where, exactly, will we live? I don't want to move out of my apartment and have Rose lease it to someone else, then be without a place to live after the year is up. I really like it at 20 Amber Court.''

''Then we'll live at 20 Amber Court,'' Erik told her.

Jayne arched her eyebrows in surprise. She hadn't really thought he would suggest that. He didn't seem like the kind of man who would be comfortable in a small, two-bedroom apartment. Then again, she was just grateful that she had two bedrooms. She'd wanted two so that Charlie and Chloe would each have a place to sleep when they came to visit over the holidays—one could take the spare room, and one could take the hide-a-bed in the living room. Now it looked as though Jayne's guest room was going to be in regular use for the full year.

Which meant that she and Erik were *definitely* going to have to come up with some reason for him to be out of town when Charlie and Chloe came home. Because there was no way Jayne would be sharing a room with Erik, especially while her brother and sister were there to see it. She didn't want to set a bad example for them. Then again, she reminded herself, she would be married.

Still, it would be better to simply get rid of Erik whenever the twins were home. And seeing as how he'd described over dinner his love for traveling, Jayne didn't think it would be a problem convincing him to get out of town for a while.

Oh, dear, she thought. She really was going to take him up on it. She really was going to accept his offer.

Surprisingly, though, the realization of that didn't alarm her as much as she thought it probably should. Where was the harm? she asked herself again. It was only going to be for a year. It might be kind of fun, really. She hadn't been altogether comfortable living alone for the last month, having never experienced a solitary existence before. Her apartment felt so empty sometimes, having no one with whom to share it, except for Chloe's disagreeable cat—speaking of whom, Jayne did feel morally obligated to tell Erik about Mojo, so that he could make an informed decision in this marriage business. She wouldn't blame him if he wanted to call the whole thing off after meeting the cat.

But, if Erik did still want to go through with it after meeting Mojo, the situation could end up being ideal. Although Jayne had only known him for a short time, he was fun to be with. He had a good sense of humor, and he made her laugh. He was cute. He was kind. He was courteous. He really did seem like he'd make a good roommate. If it wasn't for that pesky Y chromosome he had, Jayne would feel totally comfortable with the arrangement.

Then again, if it wasn't for that pesky Y chromosome, she wouldn't be marrying him, would she? And Chloe and Charlie would have to quit school. So really, when she got right down to it, this thing with Erik was the perfect arrangement.

Except for its being totally nuts.

But then, what was the point of behaving reasonably if it couldn't even pay one's siblings' college tuition, hmmm?

As rationales went, Jayne realized hers wasn't the best. But the two most important things in her life were Chloe and Charlie. She'd promised her mother that she would take care of them, should anything ever happen to her parents. At the moment, the only way Jayne could keep that promise was by marrying Erik Randolph and being his wife for a year.

For one brief, final moment, Jayne told herself that what she was about to do was sheer madness. Then, in a quick rush of words she told him, "Okay. I'll do it."

He expelled a long, slow breath, and only then did she realize how much he had feared she would decline. Then again, there was sixty million dollars at stake, wasn't there? Of course he would be relieved.

"You won't be sorry," he told her.

Funny, Jayne thought, but she was already kind of sorry. For some reason, in spite of the pep talk she'd just given herself, she had a feeling this arrangement wasn't going to go as smoothly as she anticipated.

Immediately she shook the feeling off. It would be fine, she assured herself. Everything would be fine.

It would have to be.

She inhaled a slow, steadying breath and released it as silently as she could, then did her best to smile. "Well then," she said. "I guess there's nothing left for us to do except set a date, is there?"

Erik smiled, too, though his looked infinitely more sincere than hers felt. "Oh, there is one small thing we need to do before setting a date."

Jayne eyed him curiously. "What's that?"

He reached inside his jacket and withdrew a small, square box from his breast pocket. It was a box Jayne recognized quite well—the Colette Jewelry box. Ring-size, to be precise.

Sure enough, when Erik flipped it open, she saw a dazzling, square-cut solitaire mounted in white gold—two full carats, if she wasn't mistaken, and, it went without saying, she wasn't. The ring was one of the most exquisite ones they had in their collection. And Erik had bought it for his bride-to-be.

But instead of being delighted by the gift, Jayne felt sad for some reason. It was the kind of ring a man should give to the woman of his dreams, the woman with whom he intended to spend the rest of his life. And it was the kind of ring a woman should look upon as a symbol of her man's undying love for her. Her marriage to Erik was going to be a sham. Somehow Jayne felt as if she should wear a ring from a bubble gum machine instead.

"I remembered what you said about liking the square-cut diamonds and the white-gold settings best," he told her as he removed the ring from the box. "So I went back to Colette this evening, after your shift, but before they closed. If it doesn't fit, we can have it sized up or down.''

"I know," Jayne said inanely.

Erik chuckled again. "Yes, I suppose you would."

"I can't believe you remembered what I said about liking the square cut," she said softly. For some reason, she wanted to stall for time, wanted to delay putting on the ring. "I mean, we barely had a chance to—"

"Well, now we'll have a whole year to," he told her as he reached for her left hand.

But before he could place the ring on her finger, Jayne withdrew her hand, curling it into a loose fist in her lap. "I can't accept it," she told him.

He looked genuinely mystified. "Of course you can."

She shook her head. "No, I can't. It's too much. Save that ring for the real thing, the real woman."

"What? You're not a real woman?" He smiled again. "Is there something I should know before our honeymoon?"

Jayne gulped at his mention of a honeymoon, even though she knew he was only kidding. Then another thought struck her. He *was* only kidding, right? She considered his grin and decided that yes, he was. Of course he was.

She hoped.

"Of course I'm a real woman," she told him. "But I won't be a real wife. Save that ring for when you get married for real."

"Oh, I won't be getting married for real," he told her. "Ever."

His utter conviction in voicing the statement surprised her. "How can you be so sure of that?"

He shrugged lightly, without a trace of bitterness or discontent—only absolute certainty. "I just am, that's all," he said. "I'm not the kind of man who can make a lifelong commitment to one woman. I like women—all women—too much for that."

"Oh."

A cool feeling of something unpleasant settled in Jayne's midsection at hearing his matter-of-fact assessment of himself as a womanizer. Did that mean he would be unfaithful to her during their marriage? she wondered. Not that it would necessarily be infidelity, would it? Not if the people who were married didn't love each other. Still, the knowledge that he might see other women while being married to her didn't sit well with her for some reason.

"You look sad all of a sudden," he said. "What's wrong?"

"I was just thinking about what you said. About liking women too much to commit to just one."

He smiled. "Jealous already?"

"No," she denied. Though somehow, the denial felt like a lie. "I'm just not sure how much I'll like being cheated on while we're married, that's all."

"Would it be cheating if we're married in name only?" he asked.

"It feels like it would be," she told him.

"Then I won't see anyone else while we're married," he told her.

His ready concession surprised her. "You'd do that for me? Go without—" She halted quickly, blushing furiously, when she realized where the conversation was suddenly going. "I mean... Uh..."

Erik chuckled. "Yes, I'd go without," he said diplomatically.

"For a whole year?" she asked.

"Certainly. You're sacrificing a lot to help me out. There's no reason why I shouldn't make a sacrifice, too. Marriage is, after all—or, at least, should be—a fifty-fifty split with each party giving and receiving the same amount."

Jayne had always been of that opinion, too, and she appreciated that Erik felt the same way. Of course, they were talking about two entirely different things. Jayne was thinking more in terms of emotional give and take, where Erik was thinking more in terms of favors, but that was beside the point. The point was, her husband would be faithful to her, even if he wasn't making love to her. And for some reason that was a very big deal.

"At any rate," he began again, "once our arrangement has come to an end, and we divorce, I'll be through with marriage forever. So the ring is immaterial in that respect. It should be yours."

It should be hers, she translated, because it lacked meaning for him. Just as their marriage would lack meaning for him. Then again, she told herself, it didn't have meaning for her, either, did it? So they were even on that count, too.

Still, "You sound so jaded about marriage," she told him.

"Not jaded," he denied. "Just pragmatic. I'm simply not the marrying kind. Not the real sort of marriage, I mean."

Jayne nodded. Somehow, his assertion made her feel even worse.

"So come on," he cajoled. "Let me put it on your finger. Consider it the first of your lovely parting gifts."

Reluctantly Jayne lifted her left hand and extended it slowly toward him. Erik took her fingers gently in his, then slid the ring on her finger. It fit perfectly, she was surprised to see. She told herself it was a good omen. Somehow, though, she still didn't feel quite right about the whole thing.

Chloe and Charlie, she reminded herself. You're doing this for Chloe and Charlie. That's all you have to remember. That's all that's important.

Unfortunately, no matter how many times Jayne told herself that, she never did quite believe it.

Five

It was after ten o'clock when Jayne arrived home. Although Erik had offered her a ride in his outrageously expensive, low-slung, foreign sports car, something had made her decline. Citing the need to be alone for a little while, to allow the repercussions of their discussion to settle in, she had told him she wanted to walk home alone. It was a beautiful evening, as if in apology for the nasty weather during the day, and walking, she knew—she hoped—would clear her mind.

By the time she arrived back at 20 Amber Court, however, Jayne felt more confused and distressed than ever. She hesitated before going in, surveying her apartment building as if seeing it for the first time. Soon Erik would be moving in with her, and this would be their first home as husband and wife. All in all, she decided, they could do much worse.

The four-level apartment building was rather romantic, really. It had started off as a large mansion a century ago, but Rose had told Jayne that it had been converted into one- and two-bedroom apartments in the early seventies. It still claimed the original—and very beautiful—marble foyer, with a spectacular marble staircase that led to the second floor. Many of the apartments still claimed the original woodwork and fixtures and features of a bygone era, right down to the hardwood floors and old-fashioned lighting and arched doorways.

Jayne had been thoroughly happy living here alone for the last month. And she couldn't help wondering now if that happiness would continue while she was sharing her apartment with Erik.

He had told her he would have his attorney draw up the papers for the prenup the following day, and he would bring them by her apartment at seven o'clock the following evening, so that she could look them over. He'd assumed she would want to have her own attorney present for that, and Jayne had had to bite back a nervous laugh at how he thought everyone must have an attorney at their disposal the way he evidently did.

They really did come from two totally different worlds, she couldn't help thinking. Though she would certainly have someone look the document over before she signed it.

As she made her way across the foyer toward her apartment, Jayne heard the sound of feminine laughter coming from her landlady's apartment next door. She paused a moment to listen, and recognized the voices of her coworkers—Lila, Sylvie and Meredith—along with Rose Carson's. It sounded like they were playing poker. Over tea and biscuits. Again.

Jayne smiled, and just naturally gravitated in that direction. Since moving to Amber Court and starting work at Colette, she had been enthusiastically invited into the small trio of friends that had previous only comprised Lila, Sylvie and Meredith. Now they were a quartet. The Colette Quartet, she thought with a smile. And where the other three women had made it a practice somewhere along the line to have dinner with Rose once a month, they had immediately invited Jayne to partake of the evening, too. But September's dinner was still weeks away, Jayne knew. So tonight must just be one of those spontaneous girls-night-outs that came up every now and then, when the opportunity presented itself.

And Jayne discovered then, not much to her surprise, that out with the girls was very much where she wanted to be at the moment. So, without hesitation, she lifted her hand toward Rose's front door and knocked three times in quick succession.

Within seconds the door opened, and Rose smiled upon seeing the fourth member of the group. She was dressed in her typical hanging-out-with-the girls clothes—loose-fitting beige trousers and a lightweight, pale-blue cotton blouse. "Why, Jayne," she said, "you're home early."

This was news to Jayne. After all, how long could it possibly take to sell oneself out for a large sum of money? "Am I?" she asked.

Rose considered her thoughtfully for a moment. "Well, the girls did tell me you had a hot date tonight. We didn't expect to hear you come in anytime soon."

Jayne gazed over Rose's shoulder, down a long entranceway that opened up into her landlady's living room, and saw her three friends, all seated around the coffee table on Rose's couch and overstuffed chairs. And they had all turned toward the front door with identical—and very expectant—expressions etched on their faces.

Honestly, Jayne thought, they looked almost comical, making no attempt whatsoever to hide their outright curiosity. She would have laughed out loud if it weren't for the fact that she felt so strange inside.

"Is that Jayne?" Sylvie said sweetly. "So early?"

"Guess it wasn't such a hot date after all, hmm?" Meredith asked.

"How did the dress go over?" Lila wanted to know.

Then she glanced meaningfully down at her watch and back up at Jayne. "Or should I ask?"

"Very funny, everybody," Jayne said as she strode past Rose, who had moved aside in a silent invitation for her to enter. She strode down the corridor to the living room, and, as always, was vaguely surprised by the modernity of her landlady's apartment. In so many ways, Rose seemed like an old-fashioned girl. But her apartment was bright white, decorated with numerous, and very colorful, art sculptures and paintings. Jayne sighed heavily as she came to a halt near the coffee table, then said to her friends, "Actually, if you must know…"

"Oh, we must, we must," Lila said.

"My date went very well," Jayne told them. There. That was suitably nebulous, wasn't it? Let them make of it whatever they wanted to.

"Sit," Sylvie instructed as Jayne drew nearer to the table. "We want to hear all the gory details. You're the first one of us who's had a date in a long time. We want to live vicariously through you."

"Speak for yourself," Meredith said. "I'm perfectly content not to date."

"Yeah, yeah, yeah," Lila muttered. "Just wait till the right man comes along. You'll change your tune. Pronto."

Meredith opened her mouth to respond to Lila's assurance—probably in contradiction, Jayne couldn't help but think—but Rose interceded.

"Now, girls," she said, "maybe Jayne doesn't want to share all the, as you called them, gory details. From what I gather, this is a new man in her life. She may want to keep him to herself for a while."

Something about the way Rose offered her observation made Jayne think the other woman sympathized with her situation. There was someone special in Rose's past, Jayne realized then. She could tell by the way her landlady spoke. As far as Jayne knew, however, Rose had always been single. The idea that there might be one great love in the other woman's past piqued her curiosity more than a little. She would have loved to hear the story of Rose's love life, but she didn't want to pry.

Without thinking, Jayne lifted her hand to the amber brooch affixed to her sweater, the one Rose had loaned her that morning. She remembered her landlady telling her the pin had an interesting history. And for some reason, Jayne couldn't help thinking it was somehow related to the special man in the other woman's life. She had no idea why such a thought should occur to her, but there it was all the same. Someday, Jayne thought, she was going to ask Rose to tell her all about the amber brooch.

That day wouldn't be today, however, as was made quite evident when Lila suddenly—and very loudly—squealed, then leaped up from her chair with enough velocity to send it skidding backward.

"What?" Jayne asked in alarm. She took an involuntary step backward in response to the other woman's... exuberance. "What's wrong?"

"Nothing's wrong," Lila said. But she was pointing at the hand Jayne had lifted to the brooch and shaking her finger quite vigorously.

Jayne realized then, too late, that it was her *left* hand she had lifted to touch the brooch. Hastily she shoved her hand behind her back, even though she knew the gesture would be futile.

"That ring," her neighbor continued before Jayne had a chance to respond one way or another. "That humongous chunk of ice you're wearing. You weren't wearing that when you came up to borrow my dress earlier this evening," Lila added. "I would have noticed it. You had to have gotten that tonight. What's the deal, Jayne? If you ask me, that looks like an *engagement* ring."

Oh, dear, Jayne thought. She really hadn't intended to tell her friends about her impending marriage just yet. She'd hoped to have a day or two to get used to the idea herself. Not that she could have put off announcing it for very long, seeing as how Erik had to be married within two weeks' time. In fact, it really wasn't until this very moment that Jayne even fully considered the fact that she was going to have to tell *everyone*—including Chloe and Charlie—that she would soon be a married woman. And, seeing as how she hadn't even been dating anyone, explaining a sudden engagement was going to be just a *tad* difficult for her to do.

"Uuummm," she began eloquently.

"It *is* an engagement ring," Meredith said, grinning. "From the Colette collection, no less. I'd recognize that setting anywhere. I did, after all, design it."

"And a lovely design it is, too," Jayne said quickly, hoping to change the subject.

No such luck.

"Jayne, is there something you've been meaning to tell us?" Sylvie asked, also smiling. "Like, oh, I don't know... Maybe that you've been keeping some hunka hunka burnin' love under wraps somewhere? Is he a high school sweetheart you just never mentioned to us? Or is he a more recent acquisition? In which case, darling, we want to know *all* about this whirlwind romance."

"Hey, we want to hear about it even if he's someone you've known since preschool," Lila said. "Tell us all, Jayne."

Meredith nodded her agreement quite fervently as she said, "Pretty sneaky keeping him to yourself all this time."

Oh, boy, Jayne thought. How was she going to explain her way out of this one? She really should have thought a little further ahead before accepting Erik Randolph's proposal. Like, for instance, how doing so was going to throw her entire life into total upheaval.

Gee, hindsight really was twenty-twenty.

"Uuummm," she tried again. But again, no explanation was forthcoming. Probably because there really wasn't any way one might explain what she had done, Jayne thought. Not in any kind of coherent, socially and morally acceptable fashion, at any rate.

"Jayne?" Now it was Rose who was smiling, whose interest was quite piqued. "*Did* you get engaged tonight?"

"Um, sort of," Jayne said with much understatement.

"Sort of?" Lila echoed dubiously. "Look, with a ring like that, either you're engaged or you're not. This isn't one of those cute little engaged-to-be-engaged diamond chip sweetheart rings. This is one nice piece of jewelry."

"Yeah, this guy must be crazy about you, to drop that kind of money on a ring," Sylvie added.

"So what's up?" Meredith asked.

A barrage of questions followed that one, questions too numerous and too fast-coming for Jayne to even begin to answer them all, or to even identify who was saying what, for that matter.

"Who is he?"

"What's his name?"

"What's he like?"

"Where does he live?"

"What does he do?"

"Where'd you meet him?"

"How long have you known him?"

"How come we haven't heard about him before now?"

"Have you set a date?"

"Are you pregnant?"

"*Stop!*" Jayne finally cried.

And, surprisingly, everyone did.

"Of course I'm not pregnant," she said indignantly. "Erik and I just decided we want to get married, that's all." Then, reluctantly, because she knew it was only going to reinforce the pregnancy suspicion, she added, "We want to get married right away, as a matter of fact."

"Erik?" Lila asked, grinning. To the other women present, she added, "Girls, I do believe we have a name for Jayne's mystery man."

"How about a few other vitals, too?" Sylvie asked.

Jayne did some quick thinking. "I met him over the summer. At…at…at J.J.'s Deli," she finally said, the location of their meeting still fresh in her brain. "And we've met frequently over lunch." There. That would explain why she was home virtually every night—alone. "He, ah…he doesn't get out much at night."

"Well, then I guess we can all rest assured that he's not a vampire, right?" Lila asked playfully. "So then what does he do?"

Jayne realized then that she had no idea how to answer that. She didn't know what Erik did for a living. Only that he was wealthy. "He's, um, self-employed," she finally told them.

"As what?"

"As a, uh…as an entrepreneur." Yeah, that's the ticket, she added to herself. That was nice and vague.

"So you guys met and fell in love immediately, is that it?" Meredith asked.

Jayne nodded. "Yes. That's it exactly. There was just something between us right away, and the last month has been especially wonderful, and we both just decided tonight that we knew we wanted to be together." She swallowed with some difficulty. "Forever. So we're going to get married right away."

Lila made a soft tsking noise. "You virgins are always in *such* a hurry."

In response to Lila's remark, Sylvie chuckled, and Meredith blushed, and Jayne had no idea what to say.

"So tell us more about *him,* about Erik," Meredith said, presumably to change the subject, for which Jayne was grateful to her friend.

"I promise I'll give you all the details," she told them. To herself, she added, *Just as soon as I figure out what they are.* "Tomorrow," she added pointedly.

"Tomorrow?"

"Aw, come on…"

"But, Jayne—"

"Tomorrow," Jayne reiterated firmly. Then, truthfully, she added, "I'm really too tired to go into it all tonight. It was very unexpected. He surprised me with the ring." Oh, boy, was *that* the truth. "Everything happened so quickly. I'm still kind of dazed. Still getting used to the idea myself."

"Leave Jayne alone," Rose said mildly when the other women began to voice their objections again. "She said she'll tell you tomorrow, and so she will." To Jayne, she said softly, "I understand completely, dear. It can be rather dizzying when it happens quickly, can't it?" Her smile turned wistful as she added, "But there's nothing more wonderful than finding that special someone. Congratulations." And then she surprised Jayne by leaning forward and brushing a soft kiss on her cheek.

For some reason the gesture brought tears to Jayne's eyes. In such a short time Rose had become like a second mother to her, and in that moment all Jayne could do was wish that her own mother was here to share the news. Not that the news was anything special, she tried to tell herself. In spite of what her friends were thinking about a whirlwind romance, there was no romance, no love involved. This marriage was going to be a sham from the start. There was no reason to feel like it was something special. No reason to feel as if it were something to share.

But Jayne was surprised to discover that she *did* want to share. For some reason, her engagement to Erik *did* feel special. She wanted to share the moment, her feelings, her fears, her hopes. But in that moment she realized that there was no one in her life with whom she felt comfortable sharing those things. As much as she cared for Rose and her friends, she just wasn't comfortable opening up to them completely. And although she had family in Charlie and Chloe, there were some things she didn't feel comfortable sharing with them, either.

As her friends and neighbors clamored around her to

ooh and aah over her ring, Jayne realized she'd never felt
more alone in her entire life. And all she could do then
was wonder what it was going to be like, living under one
roof with Erik Randolph for a whole year, and feeling so
utterly alone.

They married the following Friday, with more than a
week to spare before Erik's thirtieth birthday. Due to the
circumstances, it was a small, informal ceremony held at
Youngsville City Hall, presided over by a judge who had
been a friend of the Randolphs for years. True to Jayne's
request, Erik had told his family that he'd fallen in love
with the young woman he planned to marry. And although
the Randolphs had been somewhat surprised by their son's
and brother's sudden change of mind where it came to
romantic love—not to mention a little suspicious of the
timing—they had been absolutely delighted by the announcement after meeting Jayne.

Strangely, they had also stopped being surprised and
suspicious after meeting Jayne. Erik's father had even
taken him aside at one point in the evening and congrat-
ulated him on making such a fine choice for a wife, con-
cluding with, "Frankly, Erik, I didn't think you had such
good taste."

Erik simply explained away his family's total and immediate acceptance of Jayne as being the result of their
relief that they would be keeping Grandfather Randolph's
oodles of money in the family. And he told himself that
the reason Jayne hadn't informed her own family of their
sudden engagement was a simple case of nerves and not
because she was ashamed of him or herself.

Because she *hadn't* told her brother and sister of their
engagement, Erik knew. He knew that, because she *had*
told him that Charlie and Chloe wouldn't be at the wedding today. And had the younger Pembrokes known that
their sister was getting married, they most certainly would

have been present for the ceremony. Of this Erik was certain.

He and Jayne had spent as much time together this week as they could, getting to know each other and planning their meager wedding. And if there was one thing Erik had learned about her during this time, it was that family *always* came first. Even after such a brief exposure to the Pembroke clan—and his exposure to the twins had been secondhand—Erik could see clearly that they were a tightly knit trio. Considering the loss of their parents at such early and tender ages, he supposed that wasn't surprising. But Chloe and Charlie would definitely have come to Youngsville for their older sister's wedding—had they known about it.

He told himself he understood Jayne's reluctance to announce her engagement to her brother and sister. The circumstances were, after all, highly unusual. Probably, she was having trouble coming up with a suitable explanation for the rush and spontaneity. And he told himself it was her decision to make.

Still, something about her hesitation didn't sit well with him for some reason. Even with the highly unusual circumstances, Erik was a good catch, and his family was an honorable one. It wasn't as if he was someone to be ashamed of. On the contrary, any number of women would have jumped at the chance to be Mrs. Erik Randolph. He tried to forget about the fact that three in a row had declined the offer before Jayne, and that her consent had only come about in a moment of financial desperation.

That was beside the point.

The point was that Jayne, for whatever reason, was reluctant to tell her family that she was getting married to Erik Randolph. And, strangely enough that left him feeling a little hurt.

Ah, well, he thought now, as he glanced down at his watch and scanned the judge's chambers again and wondered where his blushing bride had got herself to. At least

Jayne had told her friends about their nuptials. Because
three of them had arrived en masse and were seated side
by side in a row of chairs against one wall, along with
Jayne's landlady, whom Erik had met earlier in the week
when he'd gone to Jayne's apartment to move in some of
his things. So, clearly, Jayne wasn't *that* ashamed of him,
if she'd introduced him to her friends and invited them to
share in the celebration today.

Of course, seeing as how Erik would be living with
Jayne at 20 Amber Court, and all of these women likewise
lived at 20 Amber Court, she really hadn't had any choice
but to tell them all she was getting married, and introduce
them to her intended. That was beside the point, too. In
fact, the point was—

The point was that here it was two minutes until post
time, Erik thought frantically, and his bride was nowhere
to be found.

Only when he couldn't put off facing that realization
any longer did Erik begin to panic. Jayne would be here,
he told himself. She would. She had promised. And she
had signed an agreement, as had he.

More important, though, Erik knew Jayne was trust-
worthy. He wasn't quite sure *how* he knew that, only that
he did. But she would keep her word. She would be here.
He knew she would.

And no sooner had the reassurances formed in his brain
than Jayne Pembroke entered the judge's chambers for her
wedding, thereby ensuring that she was indeed going to
keep her word. And not just about marrying him today,
either, as evidenced by her appearance. But also about
making the union look convincing—as evidenced by her
appearance. Because she had dressed for her wedding as
if...well, as if it were a special occasion.

Her suit was ivory and deceptively simple, with a slim
skirt that fell to midcalf, slit on one side to just above the
knee. The long jacket was cut to enhance her very curvy
figure, with satin piping edging the lapels and two satin

buttons closing the garment over a lacy camisole. Her pale red hair was knotted at her nape, and instead of a veil, she wore an old-fashioned pillbox hat with ivory netting that cascaded over half of her face.

And what a face. Her lavender eyes sparkled behind the netting, her cheeks were tinted with pink, and her mouth was kissed by a shade of berry he wasn't entirely certain was the result of cosmetics. Heightened awareness, he was sure, was as much responsible for her dazzling glow as was anything purchased at a department store.

All in all, Erik found her ensemble charming. Almost as charming as the woman who was wearing it. And out of nowhere, he experienced a sudden—and astonishingly intense—desire to help her take it off.

Well, well, well. It was going to be an interesting wedding day. And an even more interesting wedding night.

She crossed the length of the room to where Erik stood by himself, enjoying a final moment of solitude before joining his life—however temporarily—to another.

"I'm sorry I'm late," she said a little breathlessly. "I don't know where the morning went. Time just got away from me somehow."

"Well, you're here now, and that's all that matters," he told her. Then he smiled. "I have something for you."

She smiled back, her surprise—and her curious pleasure—obvious. "Something for me? What?"

He turned to the square white box he had placed on a chair behind him when he'd arrived, opened it and withdrew a bouquet of perfect white roses and sweetheart ivy. Then he turned and extended it toward Jayne.

"Oh, Erik," she said, her smile softening, her features turning even more lovely. "It's beautiful. I didn't even think about flowers."

He watched as she fingered the delicate blossoms with much care, then lifted the bouquet to her nose to savor the luscious, intoxicating aroma. The beauty of the flowers paled in comparison to her own, he thought. She really was quite sweet. He hoped he wasn't doing her a great injustice, marrying her this way.

Very softly he said, "I'm beginning to realize that there's quite a lot we didn't think about."

She glanced up from the bouquet, her eyes wide and startled. "Are you having second thoughts?" she asked.

He eyed her curiously. "Why do you sound so hopeful when you say that?"

She shook her head. "No, it's not that. Just… If you *are* having second thoughts about this, I certainly understand. And I certainly won't hold you to our agreement."

"I'm not having second thoughts," Erik assured her immediately, unequivocally.

Her expression changed not at all when he said it, giving him no indication of how she truly felt.

"Not about the wedding, at any rate," he added.

She said nothing in response to that, only nodded almost imperceptibly. So, with one final adjustment to the white rose he'd affixed to his own lapel—he'd opted for a dove gray suit himself, one that complemented Jayne's attire nicely—he crooked his arm in a silent bid for her to loop her own through it.

And before either of them had a chance to say another word, the judge began to hustle everyone into place. And then, before he even realized it was happening, Erik found himself slipping a different ring on the fourth finger of Jayne's left hand—a wedding ring. And then he heard himself saying "I do," and then he found himself waiting with barely contained anticipation to hear Jayne echo the sentiment herself.

She gazed intently into his eyes and smiled nervously as she slid a plain gold band over the ring finger of his left hand, then repeated the words to him. Only then did Erik realize how very worried he'd been that she would still back out of their agreement. And only then did he realize how very much he had wanted her to go through with it. And not just because it would net him sixty million dollars, either.

Then, as he and Jayne gazed into each other's eyes, wondering just what the hell they were supposed to do now, the judge was announcing them husband and wife and telling him he could kiss his bride.

In hindsight, Erik supposed it would have been a good idea to rehearse this kiss at least once at some point earlier in the week. Truly, though, he hadn't really thought about what it would mean to kiss Jayne in front of an audience this way. His head had been too full of so many other things, and he just hadn't given the wedding kiss much thought. So, with great care, and with both hands, he slipped the netting back over her hat to reveal her face. Then, clasping both of her hands in his own, he began to dip his head toward hers.

When he saw the look of panic that clouded her eyes, however, he promised himself that for this first time, he would make the kiss simple, swift and sweet. There would be time later for more, he told himself, if either of them decided more was what was wanted. And in that moment Erik knew that, speaking for himself at least, there would indeed be a want for more. For now, though, he only brushed his lips over hers once, twice, three times, before pulling reluctantly back.

And then a ripple of laughter and good cheer went up around the newlyweds, and they were engulfed in a sea of well-wishers.

Somehow Erik got separated from Jayne, and he was surprised at how perturbed he was by that separation. When he finally caught sight of her, though, it was to find that she was searching frantically for him, as well, and that made him feel better.

It was odd, really. Although he had initially gone into his wife hunt fully intending to marry someone, he hadn't for a moment planned for the arrangement to be anything more than a business transaction. He had been certain that he and his wife, although housemates, would both lead separate lives. He had known even then that he wouldn't stray or be unfaithful to his vows. He'd simply resigned himself to a year's…sabbatical, sexually speaking. Turning his gaze to Jayne again, however…

Well, suffice it to say his resignation wasn't quite as strong at the moment as it had been when he'd first proposed their marriage of convenience.

Jayne was a very attractive woman. To put it mildly. And, all modesty aside, he knew he was an attractive man. They were both unattached—or, at least had been, until a few moments ago. And now they were attached in the most traditional way a man and a woman could be joined. There was nothing—absolutely nothing—to prevent them from acting on whatever…impulses…might overcome them during the course of the next year.

Or the next week. Erik wasn't particular.

Because, speaking for himself, at least, he was already experiencing one or two of those impulses. And, speaking for himself, they were damned nice impulses to experience. It was going to be an interesting year.

Or an interesting week. Erik wasn't particular.

Jayne grinned at him, then her attention was diverted by one of her friends, and she shifted her gaze to the ring he had slipped on her finger. She turned it first one way, then the other, and smiled at the way the baguettes refracted and exploded and shone back in a brilliant array of color. It was a lovely ring, Erik thought. But not nearly as lovely as the woman who would be wearing it for the next year.

Oh, yes, he thought again. It was going to be a very interesting year indeed.

And an interesting week, too. He really wasn't particular.

Six

Jayne was *this* close to making a clean escape from the courthouse with her new—*gulp*—husband, when the other three members of the Colette Quartet caught up with her and gave her the very troubling news about her wedding present. Namely, that they had one they wanted to give to her. Because, quite frankly, the last thing Jayne needed or wanted at the moment was to act surprised and delighted with a gift chosen lovingly by her friends to celebrate her new life with her new—*gulp*—husband.

Then again, she noticed as the four Amber Court denizens gathered in the hallway outside the judge's chambers—and as she watched Erik wander off to chat with his family—that none of the women was actually holding anything. So maybe, Jayne thought, their wedding present wasn't going to be all that special, and maybe she wouldn't have to act surprised or delighted at all.

"So where are you and Erik going now?" Lila asked

in a voice that was the picture of innocence and immediately put Jayne's guard up.

"Well, ah," Jayne began, hedging. "Amy very generously offered to work my hours at the store this weekend, so I guess Erik and I will just go home, back to Amber Court, and, um…and, ah…and…you know…start our life together."

"Oh, you can't start you life together at Amber Court," Sylvie told her.

"Why not?" asked Jayne, thinking the question a very good one.

"As nice as Amber Court is," Meredith said, "it's no place for a honeymoon."

"Well, actually," Jayne said, "since we rushed the wedding the way we did—we did so want to be married right away—Erik and I kind of planned to take our honeymoon later." *Much later,* she added to herself. *Like a year from now. After we divorce. In separate cities.*

"Jayne, this is your wedding day," Lila reminded her unnecessarily. "It's special. You don't want to go back to your apartment."

"I don't?"

"Of course not," Sylvie said.

"Then…where do I want to go?" Immediately after voicing the question, Jayne regretted it. Because she was certain her friends were going to reply with something like—

"You want to go someplace *romantic,*" Meredith said. —that.

"But…but…but…" Jayne began. However, no other words came to her rescue.

"And someplace romantic is exactly where you and Erik are going to go now," Lila told her. "The three of us took up a collection at Colette this week, and we got you and Erik something very special for your wedding present. It's all taken care of. One romantic honeymoon weekend, coming right up."

"What do you mean?" Jayne asked as a sinking feeling settled in the pit of her stomach.

"There's been a slight change in your plans for today," Sylvie said with a knowing little grin that Jayne decided right away she didn't like at all.

"From all of us at Colette to both of you," Meredith added—with the same knowing little grin. "A romantic weekend for two at the Sunset Inn Bed and Breakfast."

Uh-oh, Jayne thought. The Sunset Inn Bed and Breakfast was, hands down, the most beautiful, picturesque, *romantic* place within a hundred miles of Youngsville. Situated just outside of town, it was a sprawling Victorian farmhouse, which had been renovated several years ago to be a very lovely, very quiet, very peaceful—very *romantic*—getaway.

"And your chariot to take you to this romantic weekend awaits outside," Sylvie said.

"What chariot?" Jayne asked, liking this present less and less with every new remark she heard.

"The big stretch limo parked outside in front of the courthouse," Meredith told her.

Lila nodded. "The driver has instructions to take you and Erik directly to the Sunset Inn and to leave you stranded there until Sunday afternoon."

"But…but…but…I can't go now. I don't have anything packed," Jayne objected. "I can't go away for the weekend without luggage." There, she thought. That ought to settle it.

"We already packed a bag for you," Sylvie said. "And we put it in your room this morning. It has all the things you'll need for a honeymoon weekend."

"Which means hardly anything at all," Lila told her with another one of those knowing little smiles.

"But…but…but…" Jayne tried again. Oh, this wasn't good *at all*. "But what about Erik?" she asked. "He didn't pack anything, either."

"Oh, we took care of all of Erik's needs, too," Sylvie said. "Don't you guys worry about a thing."

And this wasn't supposed to worry her? Jayne thought frantically.

Oh, dear. What was she going to do? She couldn't very well tell her friends that she couldn't accept their gift. Not only would it be frightfully impolite, after all the trouble and expense they'd gone to, but how was she supposed to explain a couple of newlyweds—a couple of supposedly wildly in-love newlyweds, so wildly in love that they hadn't been able to wait a moment longer to get married—who didn't want to spend the weekend alone together at a romantic little getaway like the Sunset Inn, compliments of someone else?

"I, uh…" Jayne sighed fitfully and gave up trying. What was the point? There was no way she was going to be able to talk her way out of this one. "Thanks," she said, trying to sound convincing. "Thanks a lot, you guys. It was very…thoughtful of you. And…and very sweet, too."

She smiled, and somehow managed to make the gesture look sincere. She knew it looked sincere, because, strangely, it felt sincere. What Lila, Sylvie and Meredith had done *was* very thoughtful. Very sweet. It showed her how much they cared about her, even having known her only a month. Good friends, Jayne knew, were hard to come by. She wasn't about to risk losing them over a thoughtful, sweet gesture like this.

"Thanks," she said again. "I'm sure Erik will be as surprised and delighted as I am."

Oh, boy, was Erik delighted, Jayne thought as they entered their room at the Sunset Inn and he closed the door behind them. Way too delighted, in her opinion. When she'd told him what her friends had done, he had chuckled with what sounded like genuine satisfaction, and his expression had turned positively sublime. And now, as he looked around their room, his expression grew even more wistful, more wicked, more...wanton?

Uh-oh.

Oh, surely she was only imagining things in her nervousness, Jayne told herself. Why on earth would Erik look wistful? Wicked? Wanton? He barely knew her.

Though the Sunset Inn truly was romantic, Jayne had to admit. Romantic enough to generate wistful, wicked, wanton thoughts in anyone. Except her, of course. No way would she ever feel wistful, wicked or wanton. Not around Erik, at any rate. No, she'd only feel those things for the man with whom she fell in love someday. And that man most assuredly was *not* Erik Randolph. Because when Jayne fell in love, it would be with a man who could make a lifelong commitment to her. Erik had made clear his inability to do that. Husband—*gulp*—or not, there would be no wistful, wicked wantonness in this arrangement.

None.

What Jayne felt winding through her own body just then was something else entirely. Even if it *did* feel just a tad wistful, wicked, and—she might as well admit it— wanton.

It was nervousness, that was all, she assured herself again. With his silky sable hair and espresso eyes, and that way he had of looking at a woman as if she were the most desirable creature on the planet, Erik Randolph would inspire that kind of reaction in any woman. And Jayne, being the inexperienced sort that she was, would be in no way immune.

And besides, their room *was* awfully romantic. Situated on the second floor of the three-story structure, it overlooked the garden in back and a lovely pond beyond. After that came rolling green hills as far as the eye could see, beneath a flawless, bright blue sky. The furnishings within were turn-of-the century antiques, with a huge hooked rug spanning a good bit of the hardwood flooring. There was a mahogany chest of drawers pushed into one corner, with an ornate, scrollwork mirror hanging above it. A marble-topped table boasting a massive and sweet-smelling bouquet of flowers was situated beneath the window, an old-fashioned rocking chair placed beside it. A charming cheval mirror stood in another corner, and at the center of it all…

At the center of it all was a quite lovely—if rather troubling—four-poster bed.

It was at that last piece of furniture that Jayne couldn't help staring. Because it, too, was turn-of-the-century, and not even close to its more modern, queen-size counterparts when it came to accommodating two people. No, two people in that bed would definitely need to know each other *very* well. And care for each other *very* much. Because they'd be squished *very* closely together, whether they liked it or not.

And somewhere deep down inside Jayne, as she pondered the dimensions of that bed—and also as she recalled all that previously mentioned wistfulness, wickedness and wantonness—she realized she wouldn't quite be telling the truth if she said she wouldn't like being squished close to Erik Randolph. The problem was, she just didn't think she knew him well enough for…squishing.

Gee, she really wished she'd brought a book to read this weekend. Preferably one where there was absolutely no squishing going on.

"Wow, this place is incredible," Erik said, dispelling—for now, anyway—her less-than-comforting thoughts. "Your friends must care about you very much to give you a gift like this."

Jayne nodded. "It makes me feel even guiltier about not telling them the truth about our situation, and letting them think we married out of love."

He crossed the small distance of the room and placed his hands lightly on her shoulders. "It was your idea, Jayne," he said softly. "You were the one who insisted we make this look like the real thing."

"I know. And I will. But I didn't realize how hard that was going to be."

He smiled halfheartedly. "Maybe we can figure out some way to make it easier."

She eyed him curiously. "What do you mean?"

He shrugged, but somehow the gesture didn't look anywhere near careless. "We have a whole year to figure it out, don't we? And a whole weekend ahead of us to get a jump start on it."

Hmm, Jayne thought. She wasn't sure she liked the sound of that jump start business.

"And I do appreciate what you're doing for me, Jayne," he added. "Truly, I do."

Jayne sighed inwardly, hoping he'd still feel that way once he realized the full extent of what Lila, Sylvie and Meredith had done. Once he opened up the bag they'd packed for him, and realized that the two of them would be spending the weekend here like two newlyweds, he might not feel so appreciative.

Or, worse, she thought, he'd feel *very* appreciative.

As if reading her mind, he asked suddenly, "So... where are these bags that your friends said they packed for us?"

Jayne pointed to the two bags she'd noticed when they first entered the room. The two *small* bags. "That must be them over there."

Erik eyed the two—small—bags with much interest, then strode toward them. "I'll assume the flowered one is for you," he said, extending that—small—bag toward her. "And that the leather one is mine," he added, lifting that—small—bag into his other hand.

With no small reluctance, Jayne retrieved hers from him and moved to the bed to open it. And, just as she'd feared, she found it filled with the sort of things a bride would need for her wedding night. Assuming, of course, that the bride in question had married for something other than college tuition for her siblings.

Like maybe if the bride in question had married for love, for example, Jayne thought as she withdrew a bottle of very nice Merlot and two slender tapers fixed in two silver candlesticks. Or maybe if the bride had married for passion, she thought further as she withdrew a mere wisp of black lace that she suspected was meant to be a garment of some kind. Oh, yes. Her friends had certainly been thoughtful when packing this bag. There was no question what that little wisp of black lace was supposed to generate.

Thankfully, there were other garments in addition to the little black lacy one. However, few of them were any more substantial. The only one that would cover her reasonably well was a silky red number with spaghetti straps and virtually no back to speak of. It did, however, fall to ankle length—but everything between thigh and ankle was red chiffon and pretty much transparent.

When she turned to find out how Erik had fared, she saw that his own assortment of what was supposed to be clothing was no more abundant than her own. But where Jayne had misgivings about her collection, he was obviously quite pleased with is own, because he was smiling as he held up and considered a pair of brief boxer shorts made of paisley silk.

"Well, I must say, your friends have excellent taste," he said as he placed the boxers at the foot of the bed and reached into the—small—bag to discover what other surprises it might hold. When he glanced over at Jayne, he saw her standing with the racy red number held up before herself, and his smile grew broader—and more wistful, wicked and wanton, she couldn't help thinking. "Oh, yes," he added in a velvety smooth voice, his gaze scanning her from head to toe. "*Very* excellent taste."

Yikes, Jayne thought. What on earth had she gotten herself into?

She tried to laugh off the tension she felt winding through her body at the sultry way he was looking at her, but somehow the nervous little titter only made her sound sort of borderline hysterical. "Um, yeah," she agreed with some difficulty. "They're, uh…Lila, Sylvie and Meredith are nothing if not, um…tasteful."

Erik was about to comment on that, but he got sidetracked by the next item he withdrew from his—small—bag, one that rather countered Jayne's most recent observation about her friends.

"Well, now here's something you don't see every day," he said as he held up his prize. "Although I've never seen one up close like this, I've always wondered what a G-string for a man was really like."

Jayne shut her eyes the moment he identified the garment, in the hope that she might not get too good a look at it. But her effort, unfortunately, was futile. Because she did manage to catch a glimpse of the red silk…gee, *pouch* was probably the best word for it, but that somehow just didn't seem to do the item justice…before she closed her eyes. As a result, before she could stop herself, an explicit image of Erik wearing the…um, pouch…popped into her brain.

"But you know, as much as I appreciate your friends' thoughtfulness," Erik added, "I just don't think this is quite my…"

"Size?" Jayne heard herself blurt out before she could stop herself. Immediately she felt her face flush with embarrassment. Oh, how could she have said that? How inappropriate could she be?

Although, she thought further, truth be told, the G-string *did* seem to be a bit, oh…largish for…well, for what it was intended to contain. Mind you, not that she had any idea what the dimensions were of the average…well, the average thing that was supposed to be contained by the G-string. But still. Surely an average man wouldn't come close to filling that thing out. Would he?

"Style," Erik said. "It's not quite my style."

"Oh," Jayne replied meekly.

"The size ought to be just fine," he added. Not that he needed to add that, Jayne thought. Not with her overactive imagination running away with her the way it was at the moment. Not that that sort of thing was what a virgin's imagination should be running away with.

Or something like that.

Well, she thought succinctly. Well. Erik must not be...succinct, must he? He must not be an average man. And why, all of a sudden, did Jayne wish she knew more about average men? Or *any* men, for that matter? And why, all of a sudden, was she thinking that maybe, just maybe, this marriage business would offer her an opportunity to *learn* more about men? Or about one man, at any rate. Which, by default, would offer her infinitely more insight into the male animal than she had now. That way, when she did marry for love and passion someday, she'd know where to begin.

And just what on earth kind of reasoning was that? she asked herself. Honestly. One would think she was sexually attracted to Erik. Then again, she *was* sexually attracted to Erik. She'd be foolish to deny that. But being sexually attracted to a man was a totally different thing than being in love with him. And Jayne had decided long ago that her first time with a man would come about because she loved him. Not because he had beautiful espresso eyes and an irresistible grin and a charming way of making a woman feel as if she was the most desirable creature on the planet.

Because that was exactly the kind of man Erik Randolph was—one who had *a lot* of experience making women feel as if they were the most desirable creatures on the planet. In fact, Jayne wasn't sure she wanted to know how many creatures on the planet thought they were the most desirable, thanks to Erik Randolph. And she wasn't about to fall under his spell herself.

When she opened her eyes, however, she knew it was too late. He was smiling at her in a way he'd never smiled at her before, with a mixture of heat and wanting and longing that only a fool could miss. And she realized then that she was already under his spell. Because, heaven help her, she wanted him, too. She wasn't sure when it had happened, or why, but sometime during the week, as the two of them had gradually gotten to know each other, Jayne had begun to recognize needs and desires she hadn't realized she had.

Her heart began to race at the realization, rushing her blood through her veins at a dizzying pace. She inhaled a deep breath and released it slowly, hoping that might steady her some.

"Ah, well," Erik finally said with much resignation, tossing the G-string thankfully back into his—small—bag. "Guess I'll just wear the boxer shorts then."

He'd just wear the boxer shorts? Jayne echoed to herself. *Just* the boxer shorts? Nothing else?

Oh, it was going to be an interesting weekend.

"Even though I really am a briefs kind of guy," he added with another one of his toe-curling smiles.

This, Jayne decided, was information she didn't need. Because now she had yet another explicit image of Erik to add to the already ample assortment parading through her head.

"But I do like what they packed for you," she heard him say further.

She looked down to find that she was still holding the red silky see-through number up before her, and yet another explicit image exploded in her brain, one of her wearing it while Erik had on nothing but his little G-string, their slick, damp bodies squished together as they writhed in ecstasy on that little bed.

"But that little black number you held up a minute ago was nice, too," he added. "*Very* nice, as a matter of fact."

Oh, my, Jayne thought. It was definitely going to be an interesting—and long—weekend.

Seven

The thought came back to haunt her only hours later, as she exited the tiny bathroom adjacent to their bedroom, amid a plume of steam and wearing the red silk—and half transparent—nightgown. True to his word, Erik was wearing the paisley silk boxer shorts for which he had voiced his preference, but thankfully not just those. Because again, thankfully, Lila, Sylvie and Meredith had had the decency to include a matching paisley silk robe, and Erik had donned that, as well. He hadn't *tied* it, Jayne noticed uncomfortably, but at least he'd put it on.

Then again, it was an unusually warm night, she told herself. So maybe his state of dishabille was simply due to him being overly warm. Then again there were lots of reasons to be overly warm, weren't there? And seeing as how the Sunset Inn was air-conditioned, and seeing as how she herself had set their room thermostat at a very comfortable seventy-four degrees, and seeing as how she

The Silhouette Reader Service™ — Here's how it works:

Accepting your 2 free books and gift places you under no obligation to buy anything. You may keep the books and gift and return the shipping statement marked "cancel." If you do not cancel, about a month later we'll send you 6 additional novels and bill you just $3.34 each in the U.S., or $3.74 each in Canada, plus 25¢ shipping & handling per book and applicable taxes if any.* That's the complete price and — compared to cover prices of $3.99 each in the U.S. and $4.50 each in Canada — it's quite a bargain! You may cancel at any time, but if you choose to continue, every month we'll send you 6 more books, which you may either purchase at the discount price or return to us and cancel your subscription.

*Terms and prices subject to change without notice. Sales tax applicable in N.Y. Canadian residents will be charged applicable provincial taxes and GST.

If offer card is missing write to: Silhouette Reader Service, 3010 Walden Ave., P.O. Box 1867, Buffalo NY 14240-1867

NO POSTAGE
NECESSARY
IF MAILED
IN THE
UNITED STATES

BUSINESS REPLY MAIL
FIRST-CLASS MAIL   PERMIT NO. 717-003   BUFFALO, NY

POSTAGE WILL BE PAID BY ADDRESSEE

SILHOUETTE READER SERVICE
3010 WALDEN AVE
PO BOX 1867
BUFFALO NY 14240-9952

Play The Lucky Hearts Game

and get...

FREE BOOKS & a FREE GIFT...
YOURS to KEEP!

Yes! I have scratched off the silver card. Please send me my **2 FREE BOOKS** and **FREE MYSTERY GIFT**. I understand that I am under no obligation to purchase any books as explained on the back of this card.

Scratch Here!
then look below to see what your cards get you...

326 SDL DC56   **225 SDL DC5Z**

NAME	(PLEASE PRINT CLEARLY)

ADDRESS	

APT.#	CITY

STATE/PROV.	ZIP/POSTAL CODE

herself could hear the soft hum of that air conditioner purring right along, well…

Well, then it was reasonably safe to conclude that any sort of extra warmth in the room, whether Erik's *or* Jayne's was *not* the result of the climate control.

Which meant that the reason Jayne felt so overly warm at the moment, as she watched Erik—in his open robe and brief boxer shorts—pulling the cork from that bottle of Merlot, and as she noted the play and dance of truly spectacular musculature on his naked torso as he performed the task, not to mention the rich expanse of dark hair scattered across his broad, bare chest, and as she observed the capable fingers handling the bottle so gently, so tenderly, as if he were taking great, great care to touch it softly, caressing the glass as if it were the most fragile of lovers he intended to take a long, long time to satisfy, and…and…and…

And where was she? She'd quite forgotten what she had been thinking about…

Oh, yes. Now she remembered. She'd been trying to identify the reason why she was feeling overly warm. It must be because…because…because… Well, because she'd just had a hot bath, that was why. Yep. That must be it. Hot bath. No two ways about it. Nosir.

That was her story, and she was sticking to it.

Jayne sighed fitfully and tried hard to pull her gaze away from Erik. Truly, she did try. But for some reason she simply could not turn her focus away from the exquisite perfection of his nearly naked body, or from the too-handsome-for-his-own-good—or her good, for that matter—features. She was just too mesmerized by his beauty of movement to do anything but stare.

Oh, she really should have kept her suit on, she thought, crossing her arms awkwardly over her own scantily covered torso. Of course, if she'd done that, then she'd be feeling—and smelling—pretty ripe by the time the weekend was over. No, best to save the suit for when she and

Erik had to go home on Sunday. Which meant that, until Sunday, they were pretty much confined to this room. Thank goodness the Sunset Inn provided room service.

Of course, that meant they were likewise confined to these garments, Jayne realized. And there wasn't much room service could do about that, was there?

"Would you like a glass of wine?" Erik asked when he glanced up from pouring his own.

She nodded eagerly. Maybe a small glass would calm her nerves a bit and help her to sleep later. "Please," she said softly.

"Your friends have good taste in wine, too," he said as he tipped the bottle over a second glass.

"They know a good thing when they see it, I suppose," she agreed.

Erik hesitated a moment, then, very quietly he asked, "So then...what was their opinion of me?"

His question surprised her. Not just the query itself, but the way he asked it—as if he were genuinely curious about the answer. She was also surprised by the fact that he asked it at all. Really, what should he care what Lila, Sylvie and Meredith thought of him? He would be seeing very little of them over the coming year. And he wouldn't be seeing them at all, once this sham of a marriage was dissolved at the end of that year. Nevertheless, it was obvious that he cared very much.

"They like you," Jayne told him honestly. "Naturally they were surprised when I told them it was the celebrated Erik Randolph I was marrying—"

"Ooo, 'the celebrated Erik Randolph,'" he interjected with a chuckle. "I like the sound of that."

She smiled. "But once they met you, I really don't think it took much to convince them that I fell in love with you in a few months' time and wanted to marry you. Allegedly, I mean," she hastily added. "You're a very lovable guy."

He smiled. "Am I now?"

Oops. Maybe she shouldn't have gone so far as to say that, Jayne thought. Because there was just something about that smile...

"That's exactly how my family reacted to you," he said, chasing her observation away. "Until the night you came to dinner at the house, they all thought I'd just run out and grabbed the first woman I could find to marry."

This time Jayne was the one to smile. "Well, didn't you?" she asked.

"Certainly not," he replied indignantly. "You were the fourth woman I asked."

She gaped at him. "The fourth?" she demanded, feeling slighted for some reason. "I finished in *fourth* place?"

"Well, I hadn't met you yet when I proposed to the other three," he told her lightly. "Had I met you before them, I'm reasonably certain you would have been my first choice."

"*Reasonably* certain?" she squeaked.

"Very certain," he hastily corrected himself, smiling that teasing, toe-curling smile again.

"Hmpf," she said, feigning effrontery. She crossed her arms over her midsection and turned her head haughtily away, tipping her chin up indignantly as she closed her eyes. "Hmpf," she said again. "I'll bet you say that to all the girls who finish fourth."

He crossed the room slowly, the soft *swoosh* of his robe her only clue that he was moving toward her. But she felt his arm brush lightly against hers as he came to a halt beside her, and she could smell the clean, spicy scent of him, thanks to the shower he had taken prior to her bath.

Sandalwood, she thought as she inhaled the sweet-tangy fragrance. There had been a bar of the soap among the effects her friends had packed for him. His scent and his warmth both seemed to surround her as he approached, enfolding her, embracing her, but she told herself she must just be imagining that. Imagination or no, though, deep down inside of her, something began to purr with delight and anticipation in response to his nearness.

Experimentally she opened her eyes and turned her face toward him a bit, so that she might consider him more fully. "Fourth place," she said yet again, this time with playful indignity.

Erik continued to smile as he extended her glass of wine toward her and cooed, "Oh, come now, Jayne. Don't be like that. We don't need to be having a tiff on our wedding night."

She hesitated a moment, then turned her entire body back to face him and dropped her hands back to her sides. Then she reached for the glass he'd extended toward her, curling her fingers around the elegant stem. "I have a perfectly good reason for tiffing," she told him. "I feel quite tiffed."

His smile went positively indecent at that. "Then I'll just have to think of some way to...untiff you, won't I?"

Oh, my.

What on earth was she doing? Jayne wondered. She was actually *flirting* with Erik Randolph. In a scandalous negligee, no less. What could she possibly be thinking? That the two of them might spend the evening in a romantic fashion? That she might actually try to *seduce* him? Then again, he was her husband, so if she *did* decide to seduce him, it would be perfectly—

Nothing, she told herself firmly. There would be no seducing going on, tonight or any night. For heaven's sake, she didn't even know *how* to seduce a man, so who did she think she was kidding anyway? Which, on second thought, was probably actually all right, because Erik surely had no end of experience when it came to seduction, and he'd no doubt be able to talk Jayne into just about—

Nothing, she told herself firmly again. Erik would no more seduce her than she would him. End of discussion.

Probably.

"So now here I am wondering," he said in a soft, smooth voice as he lifted a hand to run the pad of his index finger lightly over her naked shoulder, "what, exactly, it's going to take to untiff my lovely new bride."

Uh-oh, Jayne thought. To put it mildly.

A thrill of heat shot through her where he touched her, becoming a veritable river of fire as it wound through her body from fingertip to toe. What was happening? she wondered. She'd never felt anything like this before. Oh, certainly there had been one or two times during the past week when she'd glanced up to find Erik looking at her in a way that made her feel all warm and tingly inside, but this...

This was different. A lot different. And whatever the sensation was, it had come out of nowhere, hitting her blindside, and now Jayne had no idea what to do.

In her nervousness she abruptly lifted her glass to her lips for a sip, but in her haste, she sloshed a good bit of her wine over her hand and fingers. She groaned her distress as she began to shift the glass from one hand to the other, but before she could make a move to remedy the situation, Erik caught her Merlot-drenched hand in his own.

"Allow me," he said softly.

And before Jayne realized what he intended, he lifted her hand to his lips and began to sip the wine from her sensitive flesh, dragging the tip of his tongue gently along her index finger, then to the delicate curve between it and her thumb, collecting the wine as he went.

The sensation that shot through her then was, oh...too exquisite for words. The sensuous glide of his tongue over her tender flesh, the sight of his mouth savoring her skin with such pleasure, the intimacy of the gesture itself... All combined to send a bolt of heat rocketing through her entire body. All Jayne could do was watch as he turned her hand one way, then another, taking each finger, one by one, into his mouth for an idle taste. The damp heat enclosing her hand gradually permeated her entire body, and, involuntarily, her eyes fluttered closed. She inhaled a deep, drugging breath, hoping to steady her raging pulse, then had to release it in a quick rush of air that made her dizzier still.

When she opened her eyes again, it was to see Erik turn her hand in his, until he could brush his lips lightly over her bare wrist, and up along the inside of her arm. His warm breath skittered over her delicate skin as he went, igniting little fires everywhere he touched her.

"Wh-what are you doing?" she asked breathlessly.

He grazed a few more light kisses along her skin, to the vee of her elbow, nuzzling the delicate flesh there with his nose. "I'm trying to untiff you," he said lightly. Then he glanced up at her and, as he ran the pad of his thumb over the soft, sensitive skin inside her arm, he asked, "Is it working?"

Oh, boy, was it working, Jayne thought. She'd never felt more untiffed in her life than she did in that moment.

"Um, yeah," she said a bit dreamily. "I, uh, I think it is, as a matter of fact."

"Good," he said simply, softly, before returning his mouth to the place where his thumb was driving her mad with slow, sensuous circles.

Jayne instructed herself—quite forcefully, too—to tell him to stop, that he'd gone far enough, that now that she was untiffed, they could spend the rest of the evening playing Hang Man or I Spy or something. Somehow, though, the words never made it out of her brain and into her mouth. Instead, she only stood there, growing more and more mesmerized—and more and more aroused—as Erik once again lifted her arm to his mouth and dragged his lips higher and higher, toward her shoulder.

Erik, however, didn't seem to be suffering from the same inability of speech as Jayne, because as he brushed his mouth gently along her arm, he whispered, "You taste even better than the wine, Jayne, did you know that?"

A little explosion detonated in her belly, spreading heat throughout her entire midsection. "Oh, Erik..." she murmured.

He rubbed his mouth lightly over the curve of her shoulder, then he nosed aside the minuscule spaghetti strap of her gown, urging it down over her arm. "And you are infinitely more intoxicating," he added.

"Oh, *Erik*..."

Now he reached for her wineglass, removing it from her nearly numb fingers just before she would have let it drop heedlessly to the floor. He placed it and his own on the dresser, then turned her fully around to face him. His expression indicated quite clearly what he had in mind. And Jayne told herself she was totally unprepared for that, not to mention completely unwilling.

Until he said, "I want to make love to you, Jayne."

And then she began to have second thoughts. And third thoughts. And fourth thoughts. And—

She shouldn't do this, she told herself. She'd never made love with anyone before, and she'd promised herself ever since she was a little girl that she would be in love the first time she gave herself to a man. But there was something about Erik that made her reconsider that decision, something about her response to him that made this suddenly seem like the right thing to do.

She wasn't a little girl anymore, in any way, shape or form. She had been robbed of her innocence with her parents' deaths and the ensuing responsibility of caring for two younger siblings. And the world was a different place now from the one where she had made that promise to herself. And she couldn't possibly have anticipated a man who made her feel the way Erik was making her feel at that moment.

She and Erik *were* married, she reminded herself. Not that the marriage was real in anything other than a legal sense, but they would be together as husband and wife for a full year. Living together under one roof. Day and night. And if this was the way she was going to be feeling about him, responding to him, during the course of that year, then making love was going to be inescapable. Of that, if nothing else, Jayne was certain. It was only a matter of time until it happened. So why not just let it happen now?

Nevertheless, did she want Erik to be her first? In spite of her response to him, she'd known him a very short time. Then again, some women made love with men immediately after meeting them. It was only sex, she told herself. The most basic human instinct there was. And her husband—her *husband*—was…oh. So attractive.

She was still wrestling with her decision when Erik, evidently taking her silence as acquiescence, dipped his head to hers and covered her mouth with his. Their light kiss at the wedding couldn't have possibly prepared her for the passion and fire that was so present in this one. It was a spectacular kiss, confident, coaxing, convincing. Erik kissed her as if she were the answer to every prayer he'd ever sent skyward, as if he wouldn't be able to take another breath without her. He consumed her. He crawled inside her.

And he made her want him *so much.*

So Jayne took him, at least for now, at least until she knew for sure what she wanted. She didn't have to go all the way if she didn't want to, she told herself. She could just do a little experimenting for a few minutes and see where it took them. If things got too scary, she could put a halt to them. Erik would understand, especially if she explained to him that this was her first time with a man. She may have known him only a short time, but she was certain he was honorable. If she asked him to stop, he would.

Of course, she didn't take into consideration whether or not she'd be able to stop herself….

Nudging the thought aside for now, and acting on instinct alone, Jayne melted into his kiss, opening her hands over his bare chest, marveling at the heat and bulk of the musculature beneath her fingertips. Erik was hard in all the places where she was soft, solid in the places where she was pliant. She skimmed her hands lightly over his chest and torso, urging them beneath the silk robe and up over his shoulders, where his skin was smooth and satiny and hot.

It was, evidently, all the encouragement Erik needed. Because as Jayne cupped her hands over his bare shoulders, he let his own hands go wandering. He opened his palms over her back, scooping one down over her fanny to push her body closer to his. She felt him swell to hard, heavy life against her abdomen, and a hot fire licked at her own belly when she realized the immediacy and intensity of her effect on him.

He wanted her. In the most basic way that a man could want a woman. And something about the realization of that thrilled Jayne deep down, in a place she'd never known existed inside her. She'd never understood what it meant for a woman to have this kind of effect on a man, never fully comprehended how she herself could actually change his body, simply because he wanted her. And having that knowledge now made her feel powerful, potent, in a way she never had before.

And bolder, too. As Erik skimmed his hands down her back and over her shoulders and arms, Jayne pushed at the supple fabric of his robe, until it fell from his shoulders. In one swift move he withdrew his arms from the garment, letting it pool in a forgotten heap at their feet. Then his hands were back, exploring, teasing, tantalizing, and Jayne had free rein to follow her instincts further.

She, too, let her hands go wandering, down along the warm, silky skin of his bare back, over the salient biceps and triceps in his arms, back to the dark, springy hair on his chest, then up to the rough skin on his jaw and throat. It was a journey of newly discovered sensations, because never had Jayne been even this intimate with a man. Oh, there had been passionate kisses once or twice, but never anything like this. And now... Now she wanted to take advantage of the experience. So she did.

Erik did, too, she quickly discovered, because with every eager move she made to learn more about his body, he responded in kind. He strummed his fingertips along her rib cage, then higher, beneath the soft curve of her breast. Before she realized his intention, he covered her breast completely, closing his hand over the fabric of her gown, grasping her in firm fingers. Jayne gasped at the contact, and Erik took advantage of that, too, thrusting his tongue into her mouth to taste her more deeply still.

The dual sensation of deep kiss and palmed breast was nearly Jayne's undoing, and it was only with great effort that she managed to keep her knees from buckling beneath her. Erik closed his fingers more possessively over her, pushing her breast higher as he moved his other hand to her back, down over her bottom, which he likewise claimed with eager fingers.

She tried to murmur something—something no doubt vague and incoherent—against his lips, but she felt the fabric of her gown begin to rise then, and she realized Erik was the one responsible. Gradually, he tugged it higher, up over her knees and thighs, until he had bunched it around her waist. The hand at her breast joined the one at her waist, holding her gown at the small of her back in one fist, as he urged his other hand lower again, over the satin bikini panties hugging her hips. The skim of his palm over the fabric was an exquisite, luscious torture, but it was nothing compared to the need that shot through Jayne when he dipped his fingers beneath the elastic and touched her bare skin.

She gasped again at the intimate contact, and Erik once more took advantage of her reaction by deepening their kiss. He cupped his palm more possessively over her bottom, pushing down her panties until he had bared her completely. The cool kiss of air on that part of her that

was so seldom exposed sent a delicious shiver of anticipation through her. In response to her shudder, he dipped
his hand lower still, creasing the elegant line of her but-
tocks with sure fingers as he bent her entire body backward and kissed her more deeply still.

Jayne's knees did buckle beneath her then, but Erik
held her firm until she righted herself once more. He
skimmed his hand over the soft curve of her bottom again,
then began to tug her panties down over her thighs. Acting
on impulse alone, driven by some unknown need, Jayne
aided him in his efforts, until the mere scrap of satin lay
in a neglected puddle on the floor near his robe. Then
Erik pulled her close again, this time skimming his hand
down over her thigh. He lifted her leg up, cupping her
knee in one hand, then, as the silk of her gown cascaded
down over her waist and his other hand, he moved his
fingers over her bottom, and lower, between her legs.

And then...and then...and then...

Oh.

And then he was pushing a finger against her, inside
her, caressing the damp folds of her flesh, moving through
her slick heat to penetrate her deeply. Never in her life
had Jayne felt anything so keenly, so acutely, and never
had she been more aroused.

Not until Erik dipped his mouth to her ear and murmured explicit, erotic promises, words that made her both
blush with innocent embarrassment and hunger to hear—
to do—more. A second finger joined the first, then a third,
until Jayne went limp with wanting him. But even then,
he didn't quite satisfy her, only chuckled softly with satisfaction and scooped her into his arms.

He carried her to the bed, pushing the covers to the foot
as he lay her on her back. As easily as he had scooped
the lower part of her gown up over her hips, he now drew
the upper part down over her breasts, until the red fabric
was tangled in a circle around her waist. He lay alongside
her, gazing down intently into her eyes before covering

her mouth with his again. As he did, he cupped a hand possessively over her breast, massaging with the flat of his palm before rolling the pad of his thumb over the extended peak.

For long moments he only kissed her and caressed her, then he pulled his mouth from hers and kissed her cheek, her jaw, her chin, her neck. Lower and lower he took his attentions, nuzzling the small divot at the base of her throat, sipping and savoring the line of her breastbone, until he moved to one side and opened his mouth wide over her sensitive nipple to draw her fully inside.

The damp heat, the subtle pull, the gentle fingers pushing at the bottom of her breast to press her more deeply into his mouth, all of it combined to send Jayne into a white-hot frenzy of sensation. Never had she imagined she could feel any of the things Erik was making her feel. Never had she realized it could be this way between a man and a woman. Never would she have guessed how intensely she could want something—want some*one*. And never would she be the same again.

As Erik gently sucked her, Jayne wove her fingers through his dark, silky hair and closed her eyes, arching her body upward to facilitate his ministrations. When she did, he moved his free hand back between her legs, parting her again for his—and her—enjoyment.

She didn't know how long they lay there so joined. Time seemed to dissolve into nothingness, and the world slipped completely away. It was as if only Jayne and Erik remained behind, as if there were no other experience for her to enjoy save the one he made her feel now. And just as she thought she would slip away completely, just when she thought she would go insensate with wanting him…

He moved away from her.

At her whimper of protest, though, he only smiled. Jayne saw him smile through a vague haze of longing that blurred her vision and dulled her brain. Although she didn't know when it had happened, he was gloriously naked now, and she gazed upon his body with a fascination that bordered on awe. He was beautiful. Totally. And he was hers. At least for tonight.

"Don't worry," he told her softly in response to her murmured objection.

And strangely, Jayne realized she wasn't worried at all. She trusted Erik. She knew Erik. And she...cared for him. A lot. What the two of them were about to do felt perfectly normal somehow, perfectly right. She was glad he was going to be her first. Because she knew he cared for her, too. And she knew he would be gentle. She knew he would take his time.

"I'm not finished with you yet," he added playfully, as if he sensed her thoughts. "Nor are you finished with me. That, I promise you. But I just want to...take some precautions," he added. "Your friends were kind enough to see to that, too."

For a moment Jayne had no idea what he was talking about, only knew that she wanted him back in the bed beside her, touching her the way he had been touching her, doing all the delicious things he had promised her he would do. Then she saw him move to the bag her friends had packed for him and withdraw a handful of little plastic squares.

And vaguely, she was grateful that someone had had the foresight to think ahead. Because there was no way Jayne could have seen this coming.

"Hurry," she told him.

And, ever the gentleman, Erik was nice enough to do as she asked. Because in no time at all, he was back in bed beside her, dressed for success. He kissed her again, rolling her body toward his until they lay on their sides, facing each other. Instinctively Jayne hooked her thigh over his hip, and Erik moved a hand to her bottom again. And then he rolled some more, until he was on his back, pulling her atop him.

In her surprise, she sat up, straddling him, her hair cascading down over her shoulders and arms and breasts. She gripped his shoulders fiercely, and met his gaze levelly. "What...?" she asked. But she couldn't bring herself to say anything more. For some reason, she didn't want him to know how inexperienced she was. She wanted him to think she was sexy and knowing and seductive. Still, she wasn't entirely sure what he wanted her to do. So she only gazed at him, her breathing ragged and thready, and waited for some kind of cue.

"I want you to set the pace," he told her. "For our first time, I want you to be in control."

Well, that certainly sounded promising, Jayne thought vaguely. And not just the her-being-in-control part, either. If Erik was thinking of this as their first time, then he evidently expected this to happen again. And as far as Jayne was concerned, she could hardly wait. Still, it didn't help her with the next step.

"Ride me, Jayne," he said softly, raggedly. "Put me inside you and ride."

Oh. Oh, boy. Oh, wow.

Now she knew what he wanted her to do. But she still wasn't entirely sure she was confident doing it. Slowly, she moved her body backward, until she felt the stiff length of him pushing against her bottom. Then she lifted her hips and scooted back a bit more, until she was positioned directly over him. He smiled a *very* satisfied little smile, then reached up to cover both her breasts with his hands.

"Do it," he whispered roughly. "Do it now."

Slowly she began to lower herself over him, pausing when she felt the ripe head of him separating the damp folds of flesh surrounding the heart of her. He was so big. She wasn't sure he was going to... That she was going to be able to... But where his body came into contact with hers, a sharp thrill of excitement shuddered through her, and she wanted to know more. So, inhaling one deep, fortifying breath, Jayne rose up on her knees once again, and, in one quick, heedless maneuver, she pushed herself down over him *completely*.

There was one tiny hesitation as the barrier to her virginity was broken, and then the pain was quite intense. So much so, that tears sprang to her eyes, and she cried her distress out loud. Immediately Erik rolled their bodies again, so that Jayne was on her back beneath him, and he hastily pulled himself out of her.

Even in her pain, though, she cried out her objection at his withdrawal. "No!" she said, reaching for him. She looped one arm around his waist, splayed the other hand open over his buttock, and urged him back toward herself.

"Yes," he countered instantly, gently. He cradled his pelvis against hers, and she could feel his hard length between her legs, but he didn't try to penetrate her again. "Jayne, why didn't you tell me this was your first time?" he asked her quietly. "You should have told me."

"I didn't think... I didn't know... I didn't realize... I didn't understand..." But no more words would come, because no more thoughts would form.

"Oh, Jayne," Erik said. He brushed her hair back from her damp forehead, then bent to place a chaste kiss at her temple. "I didn't mean to hurt you. I'm so sorry."

She shook her head weakly. "It's all right. Don't stop, Erik, please. Make love to me."

"But you're in pain."

"Only a little," she told him. "It will get better now. It will be easier now." She met his gaze levelly with hers. "Won't it?"

He grinned, but there was something in his expression she wasn't sure she liked. Something almost...regretful? Now wasn't the time to dwell on that, though, she told herself. Not when there was so much more at stake. They could talk later. They would talk later. They had all the time in the world. Or, at the very least, a whole year.

"I don't know if it will get easier now," he told her. "I've never bedded a virgin before."

She smiled halfheartedly. "Then this is your first time, too."

He grinned again, and again there was something in the gesture that disheartened her. All he said in response, however, was, "I suppose, in a way, it is."

"Then make love to me," Jayne said again. "Make this the first time for both of us."

He looked as if he wanted to say something else, and she was sure he was going to protest. But he only remained silent for a moment, gazing down at her as if he weren't quite sure what to make of her, of this moment. Then, just when she thought he would roll away for good, he moved, bracing himself on his elbows, one on either side of her head. Then he lifted his pelvis from hers and, positioning himself just so, he began to ease—very carefully—back into her.

Intuitively Jayne spread her legs wider, even lifted one to wrap it around his waist. Erik uttered a soft, contented sound at that, and, little by little, entered her more deeply still. She felt tight and close at first, but he took his time, and as he pressed even farther, her body opened and stretched to accommodate him. The pain lessened with each passing moment, until he had buried himself completely within her, and then suddenly, somehow, the two of them fitted perfectly.

For a moment he only lay still atop her, gazing down at her in that puzzling fashion again. Then Jayne nodded, whispered, "Please," and Erik began to move. Slowly at first, as if she were the most fragile thing he had ever beheld, and he didn't want to break her. Then, as his own passion mounted, he began to increase his rhythm. Jayne joined him, thrusting her hips upward with every downward stroke he made, until the two of them felt as if they were joined in a way that would prohibit them from ever parting. Again and again, Erik entered her, claimed her, took possession of her. And more and more he gave of himself.

Oh. She really would never be the same again.

And then she stopped thinking and let herself only feel. Feel the sizzle of heat that slowly built into a conflagration, feel the coil of anticipation as it grew more and more taut inside her, feel the explosion of sensation as Erik carried her to a place she'd never visited before. And then...

Oh. And then.

And then a veritable explosion of sensation unlike anything Jayne had *ever* felt before. Somehow, it was as if her entire body caught fire and burned white-hot to cinders in a matter of seconds. But when it was over, she was still there, still in one piece, shuddering in the aftermath as Erik pulled her into his arms. Unable to say anything, she only curled her body against his, draping one arm weakly over his chest, nestling one leg lethargically between his two.

For long moments they only lay silently entwined. Jayne, quite honestly, wasn't capable of speech, and she suspected somehow that Erik, although capable, had no idea what to say. Vaguely she registered the feel of his fingertips as he brushed them along one of her arms. Hazily she felt the rapid up-and-down of his chest slowly lessen and grow more regular. Little by little she felt her own heart rate become steadier.

Eventually she sensed that Erik had fallen asleep, and, with one quick, subtle glance at his face, she saw that he had indeed surrendered to unconsciousness. Something in his expression, though, was troubled even in slumber. Worse, something in Jayne was troubled, too. She just couldn't quite say what.

Finally, though, sleep overcame her, too. And for that she was grateful. All in all, this wasn't how she'd planned to spend her wedding night. And she couldn't help wondering just what kind of beginning she and Erik had journeyed upon.

Eight

——

Little by little, Erik awoke to some of the most exquisite sensations he had ever experienced in his life, and he battled consciousness for as long as he could in an effort to enjoy them more. As the pink-tinted light of sunrise crept over the windowsill, he registered vaguely that he was in a bed other than his own, that the bed was much smaller and softer than the firm, king-size monstrosity he normally slept in at home, and that...

Well, well, well. That he wasn't alone.

Still feeling hazy and only half-aware, he noted that there was a soft, warm, naked body nestled against his own, her back to his front, her legs tangled with his, her silky hair cascading over his arm and her torso. Whoever the woman was, she smelled sweetly of lavender and sandalwood and some other wonderful scent he couldn't quite identify. Her round bottom was nestled nicely against his groin—oh, boy, was it nestled nicely there—and one plump breast filled his hand. Instinctively Erik curled his fingers more intimately into her soft flesh, and the woman exhaled a sigh of unmistakable contentment.

Who could she be? he wondered, full consciousness still eluding him. Although he'd had some wonderful dreams the night before, he couldn't recall acting out any of them in the real world. Where had he been yesterday? he asked himself, still feeling a bit foggy. Where could he have met such a lovely creature as she? Perhaps she was a debutante he'd met at a party last night. Or maybe she was an artist he'd encountered at a Pace Street gallery opening downtown yesterday afternoon. Or a dancer from a local premiere. Or a salesclerk from Chasan's, his most favorite store in the world. Or even a waitress or bartender to whom he had taken a shine. Or she might even be...

His wife.

Erik snapped his eyes open, fully awake now. Oh, yes. It was all coming back to him.

He had gotten married yesterday. And then he and his new wife had come to this bed-and-breakfast for a phony honeymoon. Except that last night the honeymoon had ended up being not so phony. And now all Erik could do was wonder if their marriage was going to end up being not so phony, either.

Oh, boy. This was not good. This marriage of convenience was promising to be more inconvenient than he could have guessed. And not just because, after last night, it was going to be nigh on impossible to keep his hands off his wife, but also because Jayne, Erik remembered in a flood of graphic, erotic recollection, had been a virgin last night. And now...

Now she wasn't. And he was the one who was responsible for that. And virgins had a bad habit of taking sex way too seriously. They had an even worse habit of thinking that the first man with whom they made love was special. And now Erik was worried that Jayne was going to take their marriage way too seriously—and think it was way too special, too.

Oh, this was not good. Not good at all. Never in his illustrious sexual history had Erik ever deflowered anyone. Had he known that Jayne was an innocent, he never would have taken advantage of her last night—or any night, for that matter. Not that she hadn't been fully amenable to being taken advantage of, he recalled with a reluctant—and very lascivious—smile. Not that she hadn't taken a few advantages herself, he recollected with a less reluctant—and even more lascivious—smile. Not that either of them could have in any way anticipated the fireworks that had exploded between them, he reflected with the most lascivious smile of all. Not that they hadn't enjoyed themselves immensely during the conflagration.

Especially when they had awoken wrapped in each other's arms and let it happen that second time.

Still, how had this happened?

Twice?

Normally, Erik wouldn't have been in any way dismayed that he and Jayne had consummated their marriage. In fact, he would have rejoiced in the knowledge that now he wouldn't have to remain celibate for the next twelve months. He and his wife would be able to partake of the sexual joys and pleasures that were due any lusty, married couple, then say their goodbyes at year's end with clear consciences.

But not now. Not with Jayne being previously uninitiated with regard to those joys and pleasures. Virgins tended to recall their first times with some wistfulness. Erik knew this, because he recalled his own first time with some wistfulness.

Women, he knew, were even worse about that fond recollection business. And Jayne Pembroke definitely seemed like the kind of woman who would put much too much emphasis on her first sexual encounter. She was going to think that what had happened between them last night was *important*. Whereas Erik considered it to be...

Well now, just what did he consider it to be? he asked

himself. Not important, of course, but…perhaps significant. Yes, certainly what he and Jayne had shared last night had been significant to him. But important? Oh, surely not. Not in the way it had doubtless been important to her.

She stirred beside him then, murmuring the soft, sweet sounds of a woman who has spent the night in the arms of a man who has thoroughly satisfied her. Pride mixed with Erik's concern then, along with something else he was hesitant to identify. At least he'd made her first time good, he reassured himself. At least she hadn't lost her virginity to some brute who wouldn't have seen to her needs. At least she would recall this event fondly. Wistfully. Importantly. Specially.

Oh, no.

In spite of his anxiety that he was doomed now, Erik was shaken by a profound fear at the turn his thoughts had taken, at the thought of Jayne with someone else—for the first time or any time thereafter. Somehow the idea wove an inexplicable thread of sadness through the fabric of his soul. Why he should feel that way was beyond him, but there it was just the same. He simply could not tolerate the thought of her with another man.

Get a hold of yourself, Randolph, Erik told himself as he prepared for Jayne's awakening. *She may be sweet and gentle and beautiful, but when all is said and done, she's only a woman. No different from any other. There's no reason to be getting all sappy and sentimental over her.*

He watched as consciousness gradually spread through her, noted the way she sighed her contentment and curled her body closer to his as she awoke. She lifted a hand to her hair, that soft curtain of silk that had flowed over both their bodies the night before, pushing a handful away from her face. Her eyes fluttered open then—those lambent, lavender eyes—heavy and slumberous in what was clearly a state of mind as disordered and narcotic as his own had been moments ago. She smiled sleepily at him, and Erik noted how her skin was rosy and warm and fragrant. And he realized in that moment that all he wanted to do was bury himself inside her again.

And again.

Oh, no. This most definitely was not—

"Good morning," she said softly. She launched her body into a languid, though thorough, stretch, wrapping her fingers tightly around the spindles of the headboard the way she had done the night before as he'd... Well, as he'd done so many things to her that were probably best left simmering on the back burner for now. So to speak.

"Good morning," he returned softly. "How do you feel?"

She inhaled slowly, deeply, and released the breath in a long, leisurely sigh. "I feel wonderful. A little sore in places, but..."

She blushed then, and Erik didn't think he could ever recall such a reaction in any of his lovers. Normally he bedded women who were as experienced as he was himself—or even more so. Never had any of them blushed when recalling their adventures of the previous evening. Purred with contentment, yes. Uttered erotic, explicit demands for more, certainly. And he had always happily accommodated them.

But something about Jayne's blushing now wedged its way into a part of him where he would have previously sworn he was incapable of feeling anything. It was at that moment that he completely understood what Frank Sinatra meant when he sang about having someone under his skin. And Erik realized that none of the purring or demanding had ever come close to arousing him the way simply gazing upon Jayne—all warm and naked and innocent and blushing—did.

"You know what they say about that soreness, don't you?" he asked.

She shook her head and blushed some more, and Erik went hard as a rock at seeing it.

"They say you should just climb right back in the saddle again." He smiled. "To put it incredibly crassly."

She expelled a single little chuckle, and it was almost convincing. But he could see that she was no more comfortable with what had happened last night than he was himself. Though her reasons were probably not the same as his own.

"Are you all right, Jayne?" he asked simply, softly.

She hesitated a moment, then nodded. "I think so."

"But you're not sure?"

This time she shook her head. "I don't quite know how I'm supposed to feel. Or what I'm supposed to do. Or what I'm supposed to say to you now. It's very confusing."

Well, he certainly couldn't disagree with her there. He, too, hesitated a moment before asking, "Jayne, why didn't you tell me last night that you'd never been with a man before?"

She scrunched up her shoulders in something of a shrug, but there was nothing careless in the gesture. In fact, although she was adequately enough covered by the sheet, she tugged it higher still, to just below her neck, as if she were suddenly embarrassed by her nakedness. Funny thing was, though, Erik suspected it wasn't so much her physical nakedness that she was trying to cover as it was another sort of nakedness entirely. And sheets didn't help with that.

"I don't know why I didn't tell you," she said. "I just...I wanted you to think I was experienced. I was afraid you wouldn't want me if I was a virgin."

"Oh, Jayne..." he began.

But for the life of him, Erik had no idea what else to say. Because no matter how many times he told himself he *wouldn't* have wanted her if he'd known she was a virgin, he couldn't quite make himself believe it. Somehow the knowledge that he was her first lover, the realization that no man before him had touched her the way he had… Somehow that only made her all the more special to him.

And that, quite frankly, scared the hell out of him.

When he made no effort to finish whatever it was he had intended to say, Jayne asked, "Would you have? Wanted me, I mean? If you'd known I'd never…you know…before?"

He sighed heavily and rose to rest his weight on one elbow beside her, then gazed down at her face quite openly. Unable to help himself, he lifted a hand to her hair and brushed a handful of the silky tresses back from her forehead. Then he leaned down and placed a chaste kiss at her temple. When he withdrew from her, he saw that she was gazing back at him with stark curiosity, clearly puzzled by why he had done what he had just done.

"I think, Jayne," he said quietly, "that it would have been impossible for me to resist you, no matter who—or what—you are."

And that, Erik decided then, was what terrified him most of all.

She seemed not to detect his fear, however, because she smiled shyly in response to his statement. But she said nothing further, only snuggled her body closer to his. Erik let her do it, mostly because he liked the way she felt nestled there against him, even though that, too, scared the bejabbers out of him.

He wasn't a morning snuggler. He never had been. Normally if he spent the entire night with a woman—which in itself was a rare thing—he awoke before she did and, as she lay blissfully slumbering, he dressed, dashed off an affectionate note of farewell and left. There was no mess that way. There were no repercussions, no recriminations, no regrets. This morning, however…

This morning he couldn't just dash off a note and leave. And this morning there were most definitely regrets. Not for what he and Jayne had done the night before, really, but because Erik knew it was only going to complicate what was to come. He and Jayne had a year to spend together, living together as husband and wife, even if that union was based less on genuine emotion than it was financial convenience. And before last night it had been pretty much understood that the arrangement would probably be unconsummated, and would definitely be uncomplicated. Now, however...

Well, now Erik had no idea what the situation was going to be. Not where Jayne was concerned, anyway. Speaking for his side of things, the arrangement would continue to be what he had anticipated and hoped for it to be: a year-long union during which he and his wife would enjoy each other sexually on a regular basis, then part amiably at the end of that year, both of them richer—in more ways than one—for having undertaken the experience. That, he was certain, was the way it would be for him. All he could do was hope that Jayne felt the same way, too. Otherwise...

Well. Otherwise someone was going to get hurt. And that was the last thing Erik wanted to have happen.

"Erik?"

Jayne's voice, so soft and uncertain, scattered his thoughts, and he was grateful for it. There were infinitely better things to dwell upon than what might happen twelve months hence.

"Yes?" he replied.

"I, um, I don't think we should do this anymore."

That, however, wasn't one of the things Erik had hoped to dwell upon.

"What?" he asked, certain he'd misheard her.

"I don't think we should do this anymore," she repeated.

Not do this anymore? he then repeated to himself. After what the two of them had discovered they could create together? After what had been one of *the* most satisfying nights he'd ever spent with a woman? But he had been looking forward to many months of doing this with Jayne. How on earth could she be saying oh, so casually that they shouldn't?

"Why not?" he asked, voicing his thoughts aloud.

She didn't pull back to look at him, only crowded her body into his, as if she couldn't get close enough to him. Contrary to her actions, however, she repeated, "I just don't think we should do this anymore, that's all."

Maybe he was mistaken, Erik thought. Maybe she didn't mean what he thought she meant. Maybe she meant they shouldn't snuggle in bed in the mornings anymore. Or maybe she meant they shouldn't sleep naked anymore. Or maybe she meant they shouldn't get married anymore. Or maybe she meant—

"I mean we shouldn't make love anymore."

Oh. Well. So much for that.

"Why not?" he asked again, telling himself he was only imagining the panic that began to well up inside him. "Was it that bad for you?" He had intended for the question to be a jest, but somehow it didn't sound funny at all.

He felt her shake her head. "No," she said. "It was wonderful. It was…" But she said nothing more about the incident itself. She only added, "It's not that."

"Then what?"

But still she wouldn't look at him. "I just don't think it's a good idea, that's all."

"But why not, Jayne?" he asked again, more emphatically than before.

She sighed restlessly, and this time she did push her body away from his. Sitting up in bed, she clutched the sheet tightly to her chest, obviously unaware that one small dip in the fabric revealed the lower curve of her breast, a curve Erik found himself wanting very badly to taste.

"This is supposed to be a marriage of convenience," she reminded him.

"And you don't think it's incredibly convenient that the two of us are sexually attracted to each other? Jayne, we're married, and we enjoy each other. What could be more convenient than that?"

"But accidents happen sometimes," she told him. "What if I get pregnant?"

"I'm *very* careful," he rushed to assure her. "You won't get—"

"But accidents happen," she repeated more adamantly. Somehow, though, he got the impression that the anxiety darkening her eyes wasn't a result of her concern that she might get pregnant. Jayne, he suspected, was thinking about another kind of accident entirely. He just couldn't quite fathom what.

"Condoms aren't 100 percent effective," she pointed out. "Nothing is. Except abstinence. I don't want to risk getting pregnant, only to have my marriage ending after a year. Therefore, I think we should abstain from here on out."

This time Erik was the one to sigh restlessly. "If you get pregnant, which you won't," he hastened to add, "I'll accept responsibility and provide for you and the child. You'll lack nothing."

She expelled a single, humorless chuckle. "Really."

Erik was mystified by her concern. "Of course. You and he will have the best of everything that money can buy."

Her mouth dropped open slightly, as if she simply could not believe what he had just said. "You think it's that simple?"

"Of course it's that simple."

"What about the things money can't buy?" she asked softly.

Now Erik was the one who couldn't believe what she had just said. "What are you talking about? Money can buy everything," he told her.

She gazed at him as if he had just grown another head.

"If the baby is born after we divorce, will you come over at two o'clock in the morning to feed her, and change her diaper? Will you take care of her while I'm at work? Will you be there when she comes home from school and says, 'I made Daddy a Valentine in art class today'?"

Something about that last image she described made Erik smile—though, for the life of him he couldn't imagine why. There would never be a daughter to make Valentines for him, that much he knew. And truly, he had never once experienced any desire to have children. Strangely, though, where before that realization hadn't bothered him one iota, suddenly the thought of never having children left him feeling a little bereft.

How very odd.

"Jayne," he began patiently, "I really do think you're getting way ahead of your—"

"Will you be there, Erik?" she demanded. "Will you?"

"It won't happen," he reiterated decisively.

"But what if it does?"

He sighed again, even more restlessly than before. "Fine," he muttered. Anything to put an end to this conversation *now*. He and Jayne could talk again later, when the two of them weren't feeling so dazed and confused by all that had happened last night. "We won't make love again," he lied. "There. Are you satisfied? From now on, you can stay on your side of the bed, and I'll stay on mine."

She shook her head, and the action made the sheet dip lower, and it was all Erik could do not to tumble her onto her back and cover her breast with his mouth before he buried himself inside her again.

"No," she told him, "you'll stay in your room and I'll stay in mine. Just like we originally planned."

"What?" he asked, still not believing she would go this far after what the two of them had just discovered together.

"We'll do just as we agreed to do, Erik. When we get back to Amber Court tomorrow, I'll continue to sleep in my room, and you'll take the guest room."

He gaped softly at her. "And until then?" he asked, feeling more than a little affronted. Never in his life had a woman booted him out of her bed. And this was even worse. Because Jayne was booting him not out of her bed, but out of *their* bed. "Where will we be spending the rest of our time this weekend?" he asked her. "In case you didn't notice, this is a small room, and we have no spare clothing and no means of transportation. Unless you want to call a cab this morning and risk raising your friends' suspicion when we return from our honeymoon a day early, we are effectively stranded here."

Which, of course, wouldn't have been a bad thing at all if it weren't for this silly abstinence thing Jayne had brought up.

She shrugged again, and the sheet dipped lower still, and Erik had to squeeze his eyes shut tight so that he wouldn't have to look at the exquisite prize being denied him.

"You're bigger than I am, so you can have the bed," she told him. "The love seat will be fine for me." Her words came out a bit quicker and sounded a bit more anxious, though, as she added, "And room service has been very accommodating so far. Surely they'll send up a good book or two if we ask them nicely. And I read in the brochure that they have board games available. I don't know about you, Erik, but it's been years since I played Parcheesi...."

Jayne closed the bathroom door behind her, turned on the spigot over the bath, adjusted the temperature until it was ju-u-ust ri-i-ight, tossed in a handful of scented bath salts the bed-and-breakfast provided for her relaxation...

...and then sat down on the toilet seat and began to cry.

Oh, how could she have let things go as far as they had last night? she asked herself, not for the first time since awaking scarcely an hour ago. What had she been *thinking?* Of course, that was the problem—she *hadn't* been thinking. She had only been feeling. Feeling things she'd never felt before in her life, things she couldn't have imagined she was even capable of feeling. Her response to Erik last night had come out of nowhere and hit her blindside, and she simply hadn't been equipped to handle it. So she'd let that response overtake her. As a result it had completely overrun her. And now...

Now she was a different person, both physically and emotionally, because of that response.

She'd had no idea things could be that way between a man and a woman. She hadn't come close to comprehending what it meant to surrender oneself to another person—or to claim another person for oneself the way she and Erik had last night. She hadn't realized how much it would deepen the bond she'd already begun to forge with him. She hadn't known it would, instead of satisfying her curiosity and hunger, make her curious about—and hunger for—more. She hadn't known that making love with him the way she had last night would only lock him in a part of her she didn't think would ever release him.

And that was why she had told him they shouldn't make love again. Not because she feared getting pregnant—though, certainly, that was also something to consider. But more than anything else, it was because she knew—she *knew*—that if she let it happen again, her feelings for him would only grow stronger. Every time the two of them made love, she was going to fall a little bit more in love with him. And when it came time for them to part in a year—

She halted the thought before completing it, then backed up to the one that had preceded it. She was going to fall *more* in love with him? she echoed to herself. But that was impossible. She didn't love Erik, as it was, so how could she love him *more?* Or was that the problem? she wondered further. Had she indeed already fallen in love with him? Had last night simply been proof of that? She'd always promised herself she would be in love the first time it happened. So did that mean that last night…?

No, it couldn't mean that, she told herself. She hadn't known Erik long enough to fall in love with him. Had she? Just because she found him to be gorgeous and sweet and funny and kind, and just because it felt good to be with him, and just because he made her feel happy and fizzy and warm inside, that didn't mean she was in love with him.

Did it?

The tub was nearly full now, so Jayne switched off the water and snatched a towel from the rack, burying her face against it. She didn't want Erik to hear her sniffling. He might think she was crying over him. Crying over how much she wanted a man who had made clear he would never commit himself to anyone for any length of time— unless it meant claiming a multimillion-dollar inheritance. Crying over the fact that she had lost him before even winning him over.

Because she wasn't crying over that. She was too smart to fall in love with a man who would be leaving her in twelve months' time. A man who was so earnest about leaving that he had put it in writing and signed it. A man who made clear that he would never, ever marry for anything other than convenience, and only for as long as necessary.

Jayne wasn't about to waste tears over a man like that. She was only crying now because…because…because…Well, because that was what virgins did the morning after, wasn't it?

Oh, who cared why she was crying? Jayne thought. She felt lousy. She was entitled. She only hoped this feeling didn't last the whole year. Because every time she thought about Erik, every time she remembered what the two of them had discovered together, every time she realized that it wouldn't be happening again, every time she recalled that he would be leaving her in twelve months' time…

Jayne sniffled and palmed her eyes and buried her face in the towel again. Well, it was enough to make a grown woman cry.

Nine

The love seat will be fine for me.

Those words came back to haunt Erik late Sunday morning as he and his wife—yeah, right—checked out of the Sunset Inn. There was no way he would have allowed Jayne to take the love seat while he slept blissfully—yeah, right—in the bed. So, naturally, on Saturday night, after the two of them spent the day in awkward conversation about the stupidest things—and playing Parcheesi—he had given up the bed to make himself comfortable—yeah, right—on the love seat instead.

At this point Erik felt that he could honestly say this weekend had been both the most rapturous and most annoying of his entire life. And he couldn't help but think it was just the beginning of a pattern that would last for the entirety of his marriage.

Oh, it was going to be a long year.

Now, as he and Jayne retreated to their respective rooms in her tiny Amber Court apartment, Erik berated himself yet again. What on earth had he been *thinking?* That he could simply ask a woman he'd just met to marry him for a year, pay her a large sum of money for her trouble, move in with her, with a bit of luck make love to her, and then everything would move smoothly along from there?

All right, well, yes, as a matter of fact, that *was* what he had been thinking. But that was beside the point.

The point was… He expelled an errant breath of air as he lobbed his suitcase up on the bed in the spare bedroom and began to unlatch it. The point was that nothing was going as he had planned. Something he had thought would be so simple was turning out to be anything but. And the not-planned part and the not-simple part were both looking to become habits.

The point was that he couldn't stop thinking about Jayne.

Of course, that wasn't entirely surprising, seeing as how they were married and would be occupying the same home for the next twelve months. But that wasn't what he was thinking about. No, he was thinking about how she had smelled and felt and tasted Friday night. He was thinking about the erotic little sounds she'd uttered as he'd made love to her. He was thinking about the heat and fire she had roused in him, heat and fire that he seemed incapable of squelching.

And he was thinking about how much he wanted her again.

Might as well put that thought right out of your head, Randolph, he told himself. *Because she made it clear it won't be happening again.*

And true to her word, it didn't happen again, at least not during the week that followed. On Monday morning Jayne rose and went off to work the day away, leaving Erik alone to do battle with the fearsome creature known as Mojo. Allegedly a cat, the massive black furball was, Erik was convinced, at least half panther. And it followed him about all day, he was likewise convinced, licking its chops, waiting for him to...to...to hurt himself or something, so that it could consume him in his weakened state.

By Tuesday afternoon Erik was thinking maybe it was time he took his father's advice and went to work for Randolph Shipping and Transportation. He had resisted thus far, and his father had let him, because everyone in the Randolph family—including Erik—thought him too idle and disinterested for the job. Or any job, for that matter. Suddenly, though, for some reason—and not all of it was because he was feeling like Mojo prey—Erik found himself experiencing the strangest feelings. Feelings like, oh...a work ethic, for example. A sense of purpose for another. Even a feeling of duty, and a desire to provide. That was what husbands did, after all, didn't they? he told himself. They provided. Maybe it was time he tried doing a little of that himself.

So on Wednesday morning he began work as his father's newly, if temporarily—at least for now, until they saw how things would work out—appointed vice president in charge of vague things they put temporary vice presidents in charge of. And by Friday Erik had a revelation. He rather enjoyed the work. And he was surprisingly good at it. It gave him a sense of purpose, a sense of being needed, a sense of worth. Best of all, it gave him something to talk to Jayne about at day's end.

Because, truly, the two of them needed something to talk about after spending the first week of their marriage—save that brief, erotic interlude at the Sunset Inn—avoiding each other. Avoiding seeing each other, avoiding talking to each other, avoiding being in the same zip code with each other.

Well, not tonight.

Because tonight Erik had had enough of Jayne's avoiding him. He'd had enough of her fleeing in the morning before he even awoke. Of her staying at work late, and coming home too tired to do anything but escape to her

bedroom. Of her impromptu get-togethers with her landlady and her friends from Colette. He'd had enough of
her being wherever he wasn't.

He missed her, dammit. There. He'd admitted it. He
missed looking at her beautiful face, threading his fingers
through her silky hair, inhaling the sweet scent of her that
drove him to distraction. He missed listening to her voice,
missed seeing her smile, missed hearing her laughter.
Hell, he even missed playing Parcheesi with her.

He just missed *her*. Totally. Completely. Irrevocably.
And he wanted her back, in whatever capacity she would
allow. He could make do with separate bedrooms, if that
was what she insisted upon. But he couldn't make do with
separate lives. Not for twelve months. Not even for twelve
days.

It was the strangest thing to realize. Never before had
Erik missed a woman the way he missed Jayne. Never
had he simply wanted to sit in the same room with someone, sharing her company and idle conversation. Never
had he thought that company and conversation would be
enough to sustain his interest in someone. Yet with Jayne,
his interest had not only been sustained, but had flourished. And with less than company and conversation, too.

Now he wanted more. And tonight, he decided, he
would have it.

Oh, he wouldn't force her to do anything she didn't
want to do. He wouldn't even encourage her to do anything she didn't want to do. But he wouldn't tolerate her
avoidance of him anymore, either. There was something
between the two of them that had been generated the moment they met. And in the weeks that had followed, that
mysterious *something* had only multiplied. Erik wasn't
sure what it was, but he knew it was there. He knew it,
because he saw it—he felt it—every time he caught Jayne
looking at him.

And he *had* caught her looking at him over the last
week. Several times, in fact. Looking at him as if he were

the tastiest morsel on the planet and she were a woman hungering for the merest nibble. Oh, those looks didn't last long, because she glanced away the moment she realized he was watching her. But they had been present. And they had been plentiful. And they had been meaningful, too.

And tonight Erik was going to get to the bottom of them, one way or another.

"Jayne?" he called out as he entered the apartment at just past six o'clock.

He wasn't much surprised when he heard no answer, however. He had beaten Jayne home from work every evening. Probably because of that little avoidance issue she had. Nor was he surprised when Mojo came tearing down the hallway in a black blur and hurled himself at Erik's ankle. Erik simply stepped deftly aside so that the animal went sliding past him, out into the hallway of Amber Court, looking rather foolish, actually.

Naturally, though, being a cat, Mojo recovered admirably, hopping right back up again and, with a twitch of his tail and an I-meant-to-do-that expression, sauntered back inside, plopped himself down on the sofa, and began to give himself a bath.

Erik *was* surprised, however, when, just as he was pushing the front door closed, Jayne pushed it open again from the other side.

She wore her pale-red hair down loose today, something she didn't do often, though Erik wished she would. And she was dressed in typical work fashion, with a straight, pale-blue skirt that fell to midthigh, and a snug, cream-colored top with a scooped—oh, boy was it scooped—neckline. She was wearing the yellow pin that he realized must be some kind of family heirloom, so frequently did she wear it, an interesting piece unlike any he'd seen elsewhere. He kept meaning to ask her about it, but she always slipped away before he had the chance.

He wouldn't broach the subject tonight, either, though for entirely different reasons.

Tonight it was because he had other things on his mind.

"Hi," she said as she entered, brushing quickly past him in a wide path, to avoid touching him. Her next words came out in a nervous rush, as they usually did whenever she spoke to him these days. "Sorry I'm late. Again. But I'm only home for a little bit. I have to go back out again. Dinner plans. With Sylvie, Lila and Meredith. Promised I'd meet them at J.J.'s. Don't want to miss it. Very important. There's sandwich stuff in the fridge, or, if you want, you can order a pizza."

"Oh, I don't think so," Erik said mildly.

His objection clearly caught her off guard, because she turned to look at him full on, mouth agape. "Oh," she then said, shutting her mouth again. "Okay. Well. I think there's some chicken in the freezer. Or pork chops or something. You could—"

"No, I didn't mean 'I don't think so' on the dinner selections," Erik said.

"No?"

"No."

She arched her eyebrows in obvious puzzlement. Oh, she was just so cute when she was puzzled, he thought. "Then…what?" she asked.

"I meant 'I don't think so' on the you-going-out part."

She gaped softly again, then, "Oh," she repeated.

"You've been avoiding me for the entire week, Jayne."

She shook her head vehemently in response to his assertion. Too vehemently for the gesture to do anything other than identify that whatever she was going to say next was a lie. "No, that's not true." Yep, a lie. "I haven't been avoiding you. I've just been very busy, that's all. I have a busy, busy life. I'm a busy, busy person. Busy, busy, busy."

"You've been avoiding me," Erik repeated more emphatically. "And tonight, Jayne, that's going to stop."

* * *

Jayne gazed up at Erik and swallowed hard, and, as had been the case every day this week, she had to fight the urge to hurl herself into his arms and kiss him senseless. With each passing day it was becoming harder and harder to keep her hands to herself, because her hands instinctively wanted to go to Erik. The last week had been one of the hardest she'd ever had to get through.

And, gosh, she thought now, there were only fifty-one more like it that she'd have to survive.

It didn't help that Erik was working for his father now, so that every evening she came home to find him dressed in one of those high-powered suits that made him so utterly appealing. Today's selection was a charcoal pin-stripe, which was now in a state of elegant disarray. He had loosened his wine-colored silk necktie and unfastened the top two buttons on his white dress shirt, and she watched with unmitigated interest as he shrugged off the suit jacket and tossed it over the back of the sofa. Next, he unbuttoned his cuffs and rolled them back over surprisingly sturdy forearms, as if he were preparing to undertake some very serious and difficult task.

He settled his hands on his hips, shifted his weight to one foot and opened his mouth to utter what she was sure was going to be a very stern order. He was halted, however, by a series of quick, loud raps on the front door behind him.

Much to Jayne's astonishment, however, he ignored the summons and only continued to gaze at her.

"Aren't you going to answer that?" she asked.

"I don't want to," he told her frankly.

"Why not?"

"I made plans for us this evening, and they don't include anyone else."

Yikes, Jayne thought. Fortunately, the rapping sounded again. She pointed at the door. "Well, um…I don't think we're going to be able to ignore that."

Erik didn't alter his pose at all, only continued to gaze at her in that maddening way that made her think he had big, big plans for her. Very softly, he said, "Maybe, if we ignore the knocking, then whoever is at the door will go away and leave us alone."

The knocking sounded a third time.

"I don't think so," Jayne said perceptively.

With a barely restrained growl, Erik finally spun around. Just...not toward the front door. "You get it, then," he muttered as he stalked off toward his room.

The knocking was punctuated by the chime of the doorbell, and Jayne, much to her surprise, found that she wanted to ignore both and follow Erik back to his room, ask him what had gotten into him, and hope that maybe a little of it would get into her, too, because she really, really missed him, really, really missed being with him, really, really missed being part of him. That was why she came *this close* to not answering the door at all.

Until she heard Chloe's voice coming from the other side of the door.

And before her sister could get away, Jayne flung the door open wide and squealed with delight. Because Charlie and Chloe both stood on the other side.

"Surprise!" they chorused as one.

For one long moment, Jayne could do nothing but stare silently, mouth slightly agape, at her brother and sister. Chloe's pale-blond hair was pulled high atop her head in a somewhat ragged ponytail, a few errant tendrils falling softly about her face. Her blue eyes reflected laughter and good cheer at having caught her big sister off guard.

Charlie, too, was close to laughter, his own shaggy blond locks long overdue for a cut, his blue eyes reflecting his smug satisfaction at having the upper hand on his big sister. Both of them were dressed in their standard college garb of blue jeans, hiking boots and T-shirts—an oversize red one for Chloe that was decorated with the large, entwined letters *I* and *U,* a stretched-out khaki-colored one for Charlie.

All in all, they looked happy and fit and carefree, and Jayne suddenly found herself wishing she could feel exactly the same way.

What on earth were Chloe and Charlie doing here? she wondered, nudging her unhappy thoughts away for now. Truth be told, she was very glad to see her sister and brother. She just wished their timing could have been a little better.

"We came to help you celebrate," Chloe said, as if she'd read her sister's thoughts.

Something cool and uneasy settled in the pit of Jayne's stomach at hearing her sister's announcement. "Celebrate?" she echoed nervously. "What do you mean 'celebrate?' Celebrate what?"

Chloe rolled her eyes in a way that Jayne was sure must be endemic to eighteen-year-old girls the world over. "Your *wedding,*" she said pointedly. "Which you sort of neglected to tell us about, something for which you shall pay dearly."

"Not that it won't take a while for us to forgive you for running off and getting married without telling us," Charlie added, sounding sincerely hurt by her action.

Chloe nodded vigorously her agreement. "Or for not telling us about your special beau in the first place. Jaynie, how could you?"

Oh, dear, Jayne thought. This was going to take some explaining.

"H-how did you find out?" she stammered, stalling for time as she scrambled for something that might adequately account for what she had done.

Truly, she had intended to tell Chloe and Charlie about her plans to get married. In fact, she had initially intended to invite them to the wedding ceremony. But every time she'd picked up the phone to do so—and every time she'd picked up the phone this past week to tell them the deed had been done—something had made her stop. She just hadn't known what to tell her sister and brother that would convince them she had married Erik out of love. The three Pembrokes were so close. There was no way Jayne could have hidden a love interest from Chloe and Charlie, even if she'd wanted to. They would have known she was lying.

Still, she should have made some effort to explain before now. Because now, a week after her wedding, it was going to look awfully suspicious.

"I called you last weekend," Chloe said in response to Jayne's question, pulling her back to the matter at hand, "and your friend Lila answered the phone. And when I asked her what she was doing here, she said she was here feeding Mojo. So I'm like, 'Why are you there feeding Mojo?' and she doesn't say anything for a minute, then she's like, 'Didn't you know?' and I'm like, 'Know what?' and she's like, 'That your sister is on her honeymoon,' and I'm like, 'Honeymoon? Why would she be on a honeymoon?' and she's like, 'Because she got married Friday morning,' and I'm like, 'Married? What are you talking about?' and she's like, 'To Erik,' and I'm like, 'Erik? Erik who?' and she's like, 'Erik Randolph,' and I'm like, 'Erik Randolph?' and she's like, 'Yeah, Erik Randolph—I thought you knew,' and I'm like, 'Knew my sister was marrying a gorgeous millionaire? Of course I didn't know,' and she's like—"

"Stop!" Jayne interrupted, holding up a hand as if that might help halt the flow of words. Honestly. Once Chloe got wound up and chattering, there was nothing that would stop her short of shoving half a pizza into her mouth.

"So what gives, Jaynie?" Charlie asked. "What's this about you getting married?"

Chloe nodded. "And where's the gorgeous millionaire?"

"I'm right here," a voice replied from behind Jayne.

Oh, great. Just when she thought it couldn't possibly get any worse. Now, in addition to having to scramble for some reasonable explanation for her actions regarding her wedding, Jayne was going to have to be distracted by the hunka hunka burnin' love that was her husband.

As if Erik's comment wouldn't have alerted her to his presence, she could tell he was behind her by the way Chloe's expression suddenly changed—going from simple curiosity to stark-raving awe in a nanosecond. And if Jayne had looked even half that silly as she'd stood gaping in silence a moment ago, well… Thank goodness it had only been her brother and sister who saw her that way, and not Erik.

Because when she turned around to look at Erik, she saw him smiling at her sister indulgently, as if this were the kind of reception he experienced from women all the time. And suddenly Jayne realized that the reason for that might be because this was precisely the kind of reception he experienced from women all the time. There probably wasn't a woman on the planet who wouldn't succumb in a nanosecond to his good looks and charm.

She herself had been captivated by him, if not within a nanosecond of meeting him, then certainly within moments of meeting him. And she considered herself to be a very practical person. There was no telling how many women he'd made swoon, over the years. No wonder he didn't want to bother with a blushing little virgin—or rather *former* virgin—like her.

Because he *hadn't* bothered with Jayne. Not once all week. Not that she had encouraged any sort of bothering from him—on the contrary, she'd gone out of her way to avoid him. And, hey, it had been her idea in the first place that the two of them shouldn't be indulging in any sort of…bothering, so to speak, anyway. But she hadn't thought that Erik would let her get away with avoiding him—not for long. Or, at least, she had *hoped* he wouldn't let her get away with it. And she had hoped that he would, you know, *try* to bother with her. At least once or twice.

Then again, he had told her only moments ago that her avoiding him was going to end *tonight,* hadn't he? Hmmm… So maybe he had intended to bother. Of course, with Chloe and Charlie here, that wasn't likely to happen now, was it?

Erik smiled briefly at Jayne—a smile so sweet that it almost convinced her they hadn't just been having an awkward time of it a few moments ago—then turned his attention to Chloe. "Hello," he said in that charming, captivating voice of his. "You must be Chloe."

"I must?" her sister asked dreamily, her expression still reflecting her utter amazement that gorgeous—and celebrated—millionaire Erik Randolph stood only inches away. Then, after another moment of staring in awe, she shook her head once, as if to clear it, and replied, "Oh. Yes. Oh, yes. I must be. I mean, I *am.* I *am* Chloe. Chloe Pembroke," she clarified as she extended her hand toward him—as if clarification were necessary.

"And this is Charlie," Jayne threw in for good measure, knowing it would be another several minutes before her sister recovered enough to recall the presence of anyone else in the room.

"Hi," Charlie said, stepping forward. But where Chloe evidently had no qualms about the fact that Jayne was married to a man neither of the twins had ever met, Charlie was obviously more than a little wary. Nevertheless, he, too, extended his hand, and after Erik wrestled his own free from Chloe's possessive grasp, he shook Charlie's, as well.

"Erik Randolph," he told the twins.

"I know," Chloe said with a sigh.

Oh, she really was going to have to have a little talk with her sister, Jayne thought, if Chloe succumbed to the opposite sex this easily. Of course, she further recalled reluctantly, she herself had succumbed with record speed last weekend when it came to the opposite sex, hadn't she? Yes, she'd fallen right under Erik's spell, without a second thought. Then again, once he'd started touching her the way he had, she hadn't been capable of something so mundane as thinking, had she? No, she'd had other things—other responses—to occupy her then.

Best think about that some other time, she told herself. Like when she wasn't in the presence of her two younger siblings. She did want to set a good example, after all.

"Ahhh...come on in," she said when she remembered where she was, stepping aside so that Chloe and Charlie might do just that.

And when they did, she was somewhat dismayed to see that each of them was toting a weekender bag. Bloomington wasn't that far away—only a few hours' drive—so unless they were planning to stay over—

Uh-oh.

"So," Jayne began as her brother and sister made their way into the living room, discarding their bags by the door as they went. Charlie sprawled on the sofa in that way that only overly large teenage boys seem capable of sprawling, and Chloe made herself at home in the overstuffed club chair. Leaving the love seat—oh, dear—for Jayne and Erik.

"So," Jayne began again as she took her seat there, squeezing as far to the left as she could, to put as much space between herself and Erik as she could. At this point she honestly didn't care if Chloe and Charlie found her behavior curious. "So I see you brought your bags," she finally concluded.

"Well, since the wedding was last week," Charlie said, "and since Lila told us you already had your honeymoon, we didn't think you'd mind if we spent this weekend with you." He gazed pointedly at Erik as he added, "You *don't* mind, do you, Erik? We wanted to get to know you, seeing as how we've never met you before."

Jayne sighed. Great. Now Charlie was going to be playing the part of the suspicious younger brother. This was all she needed. Especially since she had no idea how she was going to dissuade him of his mistrust when she didn't exactly trust this arrangement with Erik herself.

But Erik replied before she had the chance to, telling Charlie, "Of course I don't mind. We're family now. I totally understand your concern about me and Jayne, but I assure you, there's nothing for you to be concerned about."

Jayne nodded, hoping she looked convincing. "I know you guys are surprised. Erik and I were surprised ourselves when we realized how much we wanted to get married." Oh, she hoped God didn't strike her down for all these whoppers she was about to tell. "But it was something we'd talked about doing before, and—"

"And just where did the two of you meet, anyway?" Chloe asked, her own voice laced with skepticism, too, now that she was over her initial awe and captivation.

Jayne and Erik spent the better part of the next hour telling one fib after another in an effort to convince Chloe and Charlie that they were, in fact, wildly in love, that they fell wildly in love the moment they met and just didn't want to share that with anyone else, that they would be wildly in love until the day they died and that they didn't mind a bit if the twins wanted to spend the weekend with them, why the spare room was—

—filled with Erik's things, Jayne remembered suddenly. Oh, no. How was she going to get everything out of there and into her room without the twins seeing it? If they realized Erik was sleeping in the spare room, they'd know the marriage was a sham. And then they'd really be asking questions. And Jayne just couldn't bring herself to tell them that the reason she had married a virtual stranger was because they were all out of money, and she had been about to tell Chloe and Charlie that they couldn't go to school anymore, so sorry, but now they were on their own, good luck, and thanks for playing.

That wasn't something Chloe and Charlie needed to know about. Jayne knew they were adults, and maybe even capable of understanding why she had done what she'd done, but they were also both still kids in a lot of ways. In spite of the hard knocks they'd all suffered over the years, Jayne had managed to preserve an innocence and optimism in the twins that she didn't want to see torn away from them. Yes, she knew that they'd be entering the cold world of reality soon enough, and that she wouldn't be able to protect them from all of life's ills. But for now she could. And for now she would. Even if it meant keeping them in the dark about this arrangement with Erik.

"Um, Erik," she said suddenly, "why don't you take Chloe and Charlie out for ice cream?"

Three sets of eyebrows shot up at that. "Out for ice cream?" Charlie echoed. "Jaynie, we're not six years old."

"I know, but...but...but that would give the three of you a chance to talk and get to know each other better. And there's a Häagen-Dazs just up the street."

"But what about you?" Chloe said. "You should come, too."

Jayne shook her head fiercely. "No, I'll stay here. I have some, um, things to do. I want to *tidy up the spare room*," she said, focusing her gaze intently on Erik's, "before Chloe puts her things in there."

"Oh, I'll help you," Chloe said, standing.

"No!" Jayne cried.

Again, three sets of eyebrows shot up, but where her sister and brother were gazing at her in outright concern, Erik, at least, was getting the gist of things. Because he nodded at Jayne and said, "Ice cream sounds like a great idea, kids."

Oh, great, Jayne thought. Now he sounded like Ward Cleaver. What next? Would he be smoking a pipe? Donning sweaters with elbow patches? Telling them what a bad influence that Eddie Haskell was?

"Well," Chloe said, clearly wavering.

"They have chocolate peanut-butter cup," Jayne said, knowing that was her sister's favorite.

"Okay," Chloe conceded readily.

"You, too, Charlie," Jayne said. "You guys will have fun, I know it."

Charlie didn't look anywhere near convinced, but he pushed himself up from the couch and strode after Chloe and Erik. "We won't be long," he told his sister as he went.

And for the first time that day, Jayne was confident that something, at least, was true.

Ten

It was after midnight when Jayne finally forced herself to go to bed. She used the excuse for as long as she could of wanting to catch up with Chloe and Charlie, and only when Chloe and Charlie themselves pointedly told Jayne that they were exhausted and wanted to turn in did she reluctantly retreat to her—her and Erik's, at least for the weekend—room.

He seemed to overpower the gentle femininity of the place with his utterly masculine presence, looking incongruous amid the Queen Anne style furnishings and the soft floral patterns, the lace curtains and the poofy cushions. He was already in bed when she entered, sitting on top of the turned-down, quilted coverlet with his pillow propped behind his back, reading a business journal of some kind. He wore only a pair of chocolate-brown silk pajama bottoms, and for some strange reason, Jayne found herself thinking his bare feet were very sexy. She smiled in spite of her nervousness.

Until Erik glanced up and saw her gazing at him. Until he dropped the magazine into his lap, threw her a decidedly lascivious look and patted the bed beside him. "Finally coming to bed, dear?" he asked in a voice that was also decidedly lascivious.

And Jayne was thankful then that she'd had the foresight to dress in a pair of massive flannel jammies that were decorated with various breakfast foods, in spite of the fact that she'd had to turn on the air conditioner, because it was unseasonably warm outside.

Hey, that air conditioner could get pret-ty chilly sometimes, she reminded herself. No need to go courting pneumonia. Among other things.

"I, ah…" she began eloquently. But no other words emerged to help her out.

"Come to bed, Jayne," Erik prodded gently.

Gulp.

"I…I…I… Okay," she finally said, knowing her only alternative was to flee back into the living room and/or points beyond, something that would surely rouse Charlie and Chloe's curiosity, if not their total alarm. "I'll, um…I'll just come to bed, why don't I?"

He smiled, then patted the mattress invitingly again. "Excellent idea. Wish I'd thought of it."

Slowly Jayne moved in that direction, but with every step she took the bed seemed to grow smaller and smaller. Finally she stood beside her empty half of the mattress and realized she had no choice but to sit down. Then lie down. Next to Erik. Who was half-naked. And had sexy feet.

Trying not to think about Erik—or his feet—she perched precariously on the bed, then pulled up her legs, first one, then the other, and tucked them beneath the covers. She scrunched herself over to the veriest edge of the mattress, as far as she could without falling off. Then she lay silently on her back gazing up at the ceiling, waiting to see what Erik would do.

What Erik did was toss his journal to the floor, tuck himself under the covers, too, then push his body way farther over the halfway mark than was even arguable. Jayne's heart began to beat a rapid-fire tattoo against her rib cage as he turned onto his side—arcing one arm over her head and balancing himself with his hand flat on the mattress beside her—then gazed intently down at her. She had to battle the urge to pull the sheet up over her head, and instead only gazed back at him, helpless to do anything else.

And then, very, very softly, he said, "You, um, you have cats on your sheets."

Somehow that wasn't what she had expected him to say. In spite of her surprise, however, she said "I like cats. Well, except for Mojo. But that's only because he doesn't like me," she added hastily in her defense. "He started it."

Erik smiled indulgently. "I've never slept on cat sheets before," he said. Then he eyed her attire—what little he could see, seeing as how she'd pulled the blanket snugly up over her torso—with clear amusement. "Nor have I ever seen a woman wear anything quite like that to bed."

"Hey, women wear stuff like this to bed all the time," Jayne assured him. "To their own bed, anyway. You've just never seen it with the women you've been to bed with, because the women you've been to bed with always have something else in mind besides sleeping in their bed when they go to bed with you." Realizing how hysterical she was beginning to sound, she added, "Or something like that."

"Don't tell me you don't have that in mind, too," he replied. Lasciviously, if she wasn't mistaken.

She blushed. Well, of course she *did* have that in mind—who wouldn't?—just not the way he thought she had it in mind. She was thinking how determined she was to avoid it, and he was obviously thinking how determined he was to—

"I like Chloe and Charlie," he said, surprising her again. "They're good kids."

She nodded, feeling relief wind through her body. Maybe Erik wasn't going to make this difficult, after all. Maybe he felt as awkward as she did. Maybe he was as disinclined to exacerbate the problem as she was. "Yes. They are good kids," she agreed.

"I can see why you're so devoted to them."

"They deserve the best," she said.

Erik's smile softened some. "Seems to me that's exactly what they have in you."

Something inside her melted and grew warm at the way he looked at her then. Not because the look was sexually charged, but because it was so affectionate. And that, more than anything, put Jayne on her guard. Sex was something she was sure—well, pretty sure, anyway—that she could avoid. Affection, however, was an altogether different matter. That wasn't exactly something she wanted to avoid. Actually, it was something she *couldn't* avoid. Because she herself already felt loads of affection for Erik.

He bent and brushed a soft, chaste kiss over her lips, then rolled back over to his side of the bed to switch off the lamp. In the darkness she could barely make out Erik's outline as he resumed his position beside her, again on her side of the bed. Only this time, after arcing one arm over her head, instead of balancing himself on the flat of his other hand, he lay down and draped his other arm across her torso. In an effort to brush him off, she turned on her side, too, with her back to him. But before she could voice an objection, Erik splayed his hand open over her belly and pulled her back toward him, nestling her body alongside his, spoon fashion.

And, *oh,* did that feel good. So good, she decided not to object after all. Not just yet.

"I was thinking," he said quietly, his voice a soft murmur just above her ear, "that since your brother and sister are here in town, maybe we could arrange something with my family on Sunday. It *is* my birthday, after all. Everybody could get to know each other that way. And I know my family would love to see you again."

Well, this was certainly interesting, Jayne thought. Why would Erik want her family to meet his? Why would he want to encourage a relationship like that, when it was destined to end in a year's time? She was about to ask him if he thought that was wise when he began talking again and prevented her question.

"I'll call my mother tomorrow and arrange it. Let's plan for lunch at around one o'clock Sunday. That will give Chloe and Charlie plenty of time that night to drive back to Bloomington and finish any homework they might have."

He sounded like a worried father, Jayne thought with a smile. Concerned that they might neglect their studies.

"All right," she told him, uncertain why she agreed so readily. Something in his voice was just so earnest, so eager to please. And maybe there was something in her, too, that simply wanted to agree. Something hopeful. Something she dared not think too much about. "If you're sure," she added.

"I'm sure," he told her. After a moment's hesitation, he added, "And there's something else I've been thinking about, too."

Jayne wasn't sure she wanted to know what that something else was. In spite of that, she asked, "Oh?"

He nodded against her hair, and the friction of the gesture set off a soft humming inside her. "I've been thinking," he said quietly, "about how much I want to make love to you again."

That was what she had thought the something else would be. And she really wished now that she hadn't asked, and that he hadn't put voice to it. Because hearing him say it, so softly, so certainly, so seductively, only made her realize how much she wanted that, too.

In spite of her realization, however, she told him,
"Erik, I thought we agreed—"

"It was an agreement made under duress," he interrupted her, nuzzling aside the collar of her pajama shirt
to place a soft kiss on her neck. "I think we should talk
more about it."

But he was clearly of the opinion that actions spoke
louder than words, because instead of talking, he opened
his hand more resolutely over her midsection, and began
to drag the soft flannel across her sensitive flesh, up over
her stomach, until he could tuck his hand beneath the
fabric and open his fingers over her bare skin.

And just like that, Jayne was on fire. A conflagration
exploded in her belly, racing to her heart, her brain, her
every extremity. With that one simple touch, Erik made
her want him. Then she realized that that wasn't really
true at all. It wasn't Erik making her want him. She'd
been wanting him all week long. She'd just managed to
fool herself until now, because she'd run herself ragged
every day to make sure she didn't have time to think about
it.

Evidently interpreting her silence as acquiescence, Erik
moved his hand higher then, up over her ribs and breastbone, until he caught the lower swell of her breast in the
L-shaped curve of his thumb and forefinger. Jayne uttered
a quick gasp of excitement at the contact, and she felt him
swell hard against her bottom in response to the soft
sound. She told herself she should object, should tell him
to stop, but somehow she just wasn't able to form the
words.

Probably because she didn't *want* to form the words.

And again he took her silence as consent. After only
the slightest hesitation, he cupped his hand completely,
possessively, over her breast, teasing the taut peak with
the pad of his thumb. Jayne's eyes fluttered closed in the
darkness, and she expelled a soft sound of surrender at
the touch. Instinctively she moved her body back against

his, growing warm and damp at the feel of his hard shaft stirring against her bottom.

She heard what sounded like a quiet chuckle, then she felt herself being rolled onto her back. Before she could say a word, though, Erik covered her mouth with his and kissed her quite thoroughly. Without even thinking about what she was doing, Jayne slid her arms up over his shoulders and around his neck, threading her fingers through his silky hair to pull him closer as he deepened the kiss.

For long moments they lay entwined, his hard weight pressing into her from above, his mouth plying at hers, his hands skimming up and down her bare rib cage and along the waistband of her pajamas. Then, vaguely, Jayne felt him unfastening the buttons on her top, and somewhere at the very back of her brain a little alarm went off, however faintly. She tore her mouth from his, gasping for air, noting only now how rapidly her heart was pounding. Just as he pushed the last of her buttons through its loop and spread her shirt open wide, she finally found her voice.

"Erik, it's not a good idea," she said, the words coming out in a ragged rush. But even she could tell she didn't mean it. Especially since she only wove her fingers more tightly in his hair and pulled him close again.

"It's an excellent idea," he countered softly before bending his head to her breast and flicking the tip of his tongue over her taut nipple. "Jayne, I want you," he whispered. Then he closed his mouth over her completely, pulling as much of her inside as he could, laving her with the flat of his tongue before sucking her hard.

"Oh…oh, Erik…" she gasped. "Oh, please…"

"Please what?" he murmured against her damp flesh. "Please do that again? Please don't ever stop? Please make love to me now?"

Jayne rolled her head from side to side as he turned his attention to her other breast, but she wasn't able to form the word *no,* which she told herself she really should say. Please…'' she only repeated, with more urgency this time.

Erik continued to suckle her as he dipped his hand lower, under the waistband of her pajama bottoms, then beneath the elastic band of her panties. Instinctively she parted her legs as he pushed his hand between them. Then she bent her knee and opened wider as he rubbed a finger between her damp folds, to facilitate his erotic exploration. Again and again, he touched her delicate flesh, penetrating her first with one finger, then a second, then a third. The friction of those movements was delicious, electric, and seemed to fill her up inside. She began to move her hips in time to his manipulation, until he growled out something incoherent against her heated flesh.

By the time Jayne realized Erik was tugging her pajama bottoms down over her legs, she was nearly insensate with wanting him. It was only with great effort that she managed to reclaim some semblance of sanity, recalling that her sister and brother were just a room or two away.

"But Charlie and Chloe…'' she said, the words emerging between ragged gasps for breath. She knew the protest was futile, seeing as how they were both too far gone to halt the inevitable, but somehow she felt as if she should make the attempt.

"Charlie and Chloe won't hear a thing if we do this carefully,'' Erik told her, pulling her pajama bottoms off her completely. "Even if they do,'' he added as he went to work untying the drawstring of his own pants, "hey, we're newlyweds. We're supposed to be at it like rabbits.'' He lay down beside her, gloriously naked now, and pulled her body alongside his. "It will just convince them of what you want them to believe—that the two of us are hopelessly in love.''

Something about his statement sobered Jayne a bit, but not enough for her to pull away from him. She still wore her pajama top, though it gaped open and left her bared to him. Erik seemed not to mind, because he didn't bother to remove it. Instead, he bent to her breast again, dragging a few light kisses along the lower curve, before moving his mouth to her ribs, her belly, her navel, and points beyond.

Jayne was so overcome by the sheer pleasure of it all that she wasn't paying attention to where he went next. Not until he moved down to settle himself between her legs. Not until he shoved his hands beneath her bottom, and gripped one buttock in each hand. Not until he pushed her pelvis upward to greet his waiting mouth.

And then she couldn't help but pay attention. Because never had she felt such heat, such fire erupting inside herself. Erik tasted her leisurely, thoroughly, as if he were a starving man and she were the most luscious meal he had ever had laid before him. Over and over again, he savored her, consumed her, until Jayne could do no more than grip the spindles of her headboard and writhe beneath his ministrations.

Little by little, her breathing grew more erratic, harder and harder, until she didn't think she could keep quiet any longer. Erik seemed to sense her distress, because finally—*finally*—he moved his body back up along hers and knelt between her legs. At some point during her delirium, he had donned a condom, and now he wrapped her legs around his waist, holding her ankles firm at the small of his back. Then he slipped inside her, *deep* inside her, entering her again and again and again and again....

A tensely wound coil inside Jayne began to curl tighter every time he thrust himself inside her, clenching so taut, she thought it would never loosen. Then, as Erik increased his rhythm, as his penetration went deeper, that spring began to unwind. As he jerked himself forward one last time, as he spilled himself inside her, Jayne, too, felt a release unlike anything she had ever felt before, and she thrust her hips upward to meet him one final time. For long moments the two of them seemed to be suspended in time, then, as if the move had been choreographed, she reached for him, and he fell forward, collapsing beside her.

She wrapped her arms around his shoulders and held him close, and Erik buried his face in the curve where her shoulder met her throat. His breathing was as frayed and uneven as her own, his capacity for speech no better than hers. Neither of them spoke a word for some time. Each waited until their respiration had leveled, their heart rates had steadied, and their bodies had relaxed.

And even then neither seemed to know what to say. It occurred to Jayne, too late, that although they had taken precautions to protect her body, she hadn't done anything to protect her heart. And something she had begun to suspect earlier in the week, something she had absolutely forbidden herself to consider, became crystal clear in that moment. And it was a terrible, terrible thing to realize.

Jayne was in love with her husband.

And she had no idea what to do.

Jayne, Erik and the twins spent Saturday together, doing the sorts of things that families did on weekends. The four of them had breakfast together at a local diner, then Erik took them sailing on Lake Michigan. They enjoyed dinner at J.J.'s, where she and Erik had gotten engaged, and topped off the evening at an outdoor concert in the park. And through it all, Jayne had watched her siblings become as enamored of Erik as she was herself. And through it all, she only fell in love with him that much more.

The birthday lunch that Erik's mother organized at the Randolph estate on Sunday afternoon was even more fun, really more wonderful than Jayne ever could have imagined it would be. Mrs. Randolph—or, rather, Lydia, as she insisted Jayne and the twins call her—pulled out all the stops. The table was set with the fine Randolph china and crystal and silver, fresh flower centerpieces and place cards. There were elegant little sandwiches cut into crustless triangles, fresh fruit and cheeses, cappuccino and mimosas. Never in her life had Jayne been a part of so grand an occasion. And it was for her and her siblings as much as it was Erik. They were guests of honor, too.

And, boy, were they made to feel like it, too. Erik's parents welcomed her and Chloe and Charlie with open arms, quite literally, hugging all three of them as they entered. Erik's sisters latched right on to Chloe, and Jayne noticed the three of them engaged in laughter and animated conversation every time she caught sight of them. Erik had made every effort Saturday to befriend Charlie, and now Charlie, her suspicious younger brother, was virtually Erik's best bud. By the end of the afternoon the two of them were chatting and laughing like old school mates.

It was nearly overwhelming for Jayne to see it all. For so long it had been only her and Chloe and Charlie, the three Pembrokes, you and you and me against the world. Now, suddenly, here was an entire family eagerly welcoming them into their fold, because Jayne had brought them into it by marrying one of their members.

Everything, truly, was perfect.

And Jayne entered a bleak, black depression as a result.

What next? she wondered. She hadn't anticipated this at all. It was bad enough that she had fallen in love with Erik herself. She hadn't expected for Chloe and Charlie— or herself, for that matter—to be so enthusiastically embraced by the rest of the Randolphs. She supposed she shouldn't be surprised—the Randolphs were known for being an outgoing, giving, warm family. And Chloe and Charlie were both utterly charming, captivating people.

Of course the Randolphs and Pembrokes would hit it off, she told herself. *Of course* they would all like each other. *Of course* they would all become friends. *Of course* they would all feel like family.

There was just one problem. They weren't family.

Not really. Not the way they all thought they were.
Except for Erik and Jayne, none of them knew they would
only be related for a year. And when that year was up,
when Erik and Jayne dissolved their marriage, they would
all be ex-family.

Would that make them all ex-friends, too? Jayne wondered. Chloe seemed to have hit it off especially well with
Erik's youngest sister. She'd seen the two of them ex-
changing phone numbers and e-mail addresses, and promising to stay in touch regularly. They both had such a
strong affinity for Marcel Proust and Gustav Klimt and
obscure dance bands, Jayne knew the two of them would
indeed forge a strong bond. If they hadn't forged such a
bond already.

Chloe had never really had a best friend before. And
she hadn't warmed up to anyone this way since their parents' deaths. And Charlie, whom Jayne had worried over
for the past four years because he didn't have a strong
masculine role model in his life, was already showing
signs of looking up to Erik the way one would an older
brother.

If things kept up like this—and truly, there was no reason to think they wouldn't, if the families were getting
along this well—then it was going to devastate Chloe and
Charlie to sever ties with the Randolphs when she and
Erik divorced a year from now. And Chloe and Charlie
would sever ties, that Jayne knew. They were too devoted
to her not to. If—when—she and Erik divorced, even under amicable circumstances, the twins would side resolutely with Jayne. They would forsake the Randolphs
completely, if for no other reason than to show their al-
legiance to their big sister.

A year, Jayne thought again. That was a long time for
relationships to cement. By the end of that time, it really
would devastate the twins to lose their newly discovered
family.

Oh, what was she going to do? Jayne wondered as she

stood in the arch that separated the dining room from the parlor, where the luncheon party had retreated to enjoy coffee and dessert. She couldn't very well shout at them all to stop getting along so well, stop it right now, because they'd all be on opposite sides a year from now, could she? Even if the divorce was amicable, there were going to be some dividend loyalties. At best, there would be some awkwardness. At worst, there would be the complete severance of ties.

Chloe and Charlie had already lost so much, Jayne thought. They were just now getting to the point where they were rebuilding their lives and moving forward with them. She didn't want to see them embrace the Randolphs with wide-open hearts, only to lose them, too.

And *she* didn't want to fall any more in love with Erik than she already had, only to lose him, too.

"Nice party, isn't it?"

She spun around to find Erik standing behind her, as if he had been conjured from her thoughts. His smile told her he was quite pleased with himself for having succeeded in sneaking up on her. He looked very handsome in his khaki trousers and deep-purple polo, his dark hair pushed back from his forehead with a negligent hand. His clothes were a perfect complement to her own sleeveless lilac blouse and skirt. As an afterthought, she'd affixed Rose Carson's amber pin to her shirt, and now Jayne reached up to stroke it, feeling oddly comforted by its presence.

She'd taken quite a liking to the brooch over the last few weeks. But she was going to have to remember to give it back to Rose soon. Surely her landlady would miss so special a keepsake.

Erik's dark eyes sparkled with something Jayne was afraid to contemplate as he watched her, and she remembered how she had awakened in his arms the last two mornings, seeing an expression very much like the one he wore now. They had made love last night, too, she recalled as a warm, fizzy sensation bubbled up inside her, even more sweetly than they had on Friday. Despite all the misgivings she'd been having about their relationship, she hadn't been able to resist him when he touched her so tenderly. And this morning, when she'd awoken to find herself nestled in his arms, when she'd felt his heart beating in rhythmic time against her own…

She closed her eyes briefly now at the recollection. Because when she had awoken to all those things this morning, she had realized how irrevocably in love with him she was.

Her heart ached as she opened her eyes now to gaze at him. He was so handsome. So sweet. So gentle. So wonderful to be with. Why couldn't he fall in love with her, the way she had fallen in love with him? Why couldn't he just love her a little bit? Why was he determined that, in a year's time, they should part ways?

Because he *wasn't* in love with her, she immediately answered herself. Not even a little bit. Oh, certainly he cared for her—that she couldn't deny. But he'd made it clear that he simply did not fall in love, that he would never tie his life to another, that they would both be on their merry ways once their obligation to each other ended. And that obligation was legal, not emotional, she reminded herself ruthlessly. More than that, that obligation was temporary.

Would that her emotions could be temporary, too, she thought, there wouldn't be a problem would there?

"Yes. It is a nice party," she finally said in response to his question. "Your mother is a wonderful hostess. It was nice of her to put this together on such short notice."

Erik nodded as he scanned the room beyond. "Everyone seems to be having a good time."

"Yes. They do."

His gaze returned to hers, and he sobered. "Except for you. Why do you look so glum, Jayne?"

She met his gaze levelly, too, sobering even more than

he. And in that moment she made a hasty—but final—decision. "Erik?" she asked. "Can we talk?"

He shrugged lightly, but somehow the gesture seemed in no way careless. "Of course. About what?"

"Privately, I mean. Can we talk privately?"

Her request seemed to bother him, because he eyed her warily. "What's wrong, Jayne?"

"I just…we need to talk," she reiterated. "Privately. Please."

"All right. My father's study is through here."

He gestured toward a door on the wall closest to them, then proceeded in that direction without looking back. Jayne followed automatically, rehearsing in her head what she wanted to say to him, then reconsidering, then changing her mind, then resolving once more to go along with her initial decision with greater purpose. By the time Erik closed the door behind them, she was becoming so confused by the back and forth and circular motions of her mind that she wasn't sure what she wanted to say.

Erik seemed to sense her quandary, because he made no move to coax or cajole her. He only strode over to his father's desk and perched on the very edge of it, crossing his arms over his torso in a gesture that seemed defensive somehow. And he waited in silence for her to say whatever it was she needed to say.

He was so handsome, she thought again. And she loved him so much. Did she really want to end their temporary marriage before she'd had the chance to enjoy it to its fullest extent? But honestly, what other alternative did she have? Every day she was only going to fall more deeply in love with him. Every day her family would grow to love his more. By year's end, her heart—and Charlie and Chloe's hearts, too—were going to be so full, that losing the Randolphs and losing Erik would be too devastating to bear. If she ended this now, perhaps she'd at least be able to salvage something. A year from now, though…

A year from now she just might not recover at all.

"I can't do this," she said suddenly. She hadn't meant to just blurt her decision out that way, but once she had uttered it, she felt better for it. Sort of.

Erik seemed vaguely puzzled by the remark. "Can't do what?"

She hesitated a moment before clarifying, "I can't go through with our arrangement."

Still, though, he seemed not to understand. He only shook his head slowly in silence, his expression clearly puzzled.

"With our marriage," she added. "I can't go through with our marriage."

That had him on his feet in an instant. But he seemed not to know what to say, because he only stood there, staring at her, his mouth slightly agape, his hands hooked loosely on his hips.

"I'm sorry, Erik," she told him. "But it's just not going to work."

He did find his voice then, demanding, "What are you talking about? It's working beautifully. Better than I imagined it could."

Oh, sure, she thought. After all, he'd married a woman with whom he could make love every night of the week and never risk falling irrevocably in love with her... because he simply didn't have the capacity for such an emotion. But there was more to a marriage—even a marriage of convenience—than sexual compatibility. The problem was, Jayne was willing—eager—to embrace that *more,* while Erik wanted nothing to do with it.

"Erik, how do you feel about me?" she asked him impulsively.

The question seemed to stump him, because he looked vaguely puzzled as he asked, "What?"

"How do you feel about me?" she repeated.

He offered another one of those not-so-careless shrugs, shook his head in mystification again, then said, "I like you, Jayne. I think you're sweet."

"Nothing more?"

He expelled a soft, incredulous sound. "Well, of course there's more."

"Like what?"

"Like…like…like I think you have a good sense of humor. And you're nice. And I like how devoted you are to your brother and sister. And you make me feel good."

"Nothing more?" she asked again.

"Jayne, just what is it you want me to say?" Now his voice was faintly irritated, as if he were losing patience with her.

She supposed she couldn't blame him. She wasn't sure what she wanted him to say, either. Except, of course, that he loved her and couldn't live without her and never wanted to let her go. Oh, hey, but other than that…

She hesitated a moment before telling him, "I want you to say that there's more to our marriage than just convenience."

Once again he shook his head in that faintly confused way. "I don't know what you mean."

"I mean…" She inhaled a deep, fortifying breath and released it slowly. "I mean…" Finally she gave up trying to explain. How could she, when she scarcely understood it all herself? Instead she only reiterated, "I can't go through with our marriage. It's over, Erik," she told him softly. She twisted her wedding and engagement rings off her left hand, then strode toward the desk and laid them down on it. "I just can't do this for a year."

"But…but, Jayne…" he began. "You promised. You even signed a contract. We made a deal."

That stupid contract, she thought. After what she'd just told him, that piece of paper was what was uppermost in his mind. He was worried about losing his millions far more than he worried about losing her. If she hadn't already been certain that he didn't love her, this would have convinced her for sure.

"I won't file for divorce until the year is up," she told

him. "Not because I signed a contract, but because I made a promise to you. And I never break my promises. But you and I—" she swallowed with some difficulty "—we'll live separate lives for the rest of that time. Please don't come home...." She squeezed her eyes shut tight at her choice of words. "Please don't come back to Amber Court tonight," she corrected herself, opening her eyes again. "You can move your things out of my apartment tomorrow. I don't want to see you anymore after that."

He said nothing for a moment, only gazed at her blankly, as if he simply could not believe what she was telling him. Then very quietly he said, "You could be pregnant. What happens then?"

She shook her head vehemently. "We've always taken precautions."

"But nothing's 100 percent, remember?" he told her. "You said so yourself. What if you're pregnant?"

"I'm not pregnant," she told him decisively. "We took precautions, and the timing was totally wrong, anyway. So you don't have to worry about it."

"Who says I'd be worried?" he asked cryptically.

Jayne wasn't sure what he meant by that, or why he was clinging to an idea he himself had so disavowed only a week ago. But she did know one thing: his reaction to her decision now was cool enough that she was sure she was making the right choice. Erik didn't love her. And if he didn't love her after those extraordinary nights the two of them had shared, then he wasn't going to love her. Ever.

"Where is all this coming from?" he asked, still obviously baffled. "I thought we were doing great, Jayne. I thought we were both going to enjoy the year ahead. I thought..." He expelled a soft sound of frustration. "I thought you cared for me."

"I'm sorry," she said again, unable to tolerate the rush of emotion that was fast wringing her inside out. "I do care for you. More than you know. And I wish I could go along with our original plan. But I can't.''

"Why not?"

"I just can't go through with it, Erik," she told him again, unwilling to give him the real reason. "I can't go on pretending to be your happily wedded wife when I'm not. I can't spend the next year letting everybody believe that we're wildly in love when that's such a bald-faced lie. I just can't do it. I thought I could, but I can't.''

"The pretending to be in love part was your idea," he reminded her.

She nodded, but the gesture felt jerky, awkward. "I know it was. But it was a mistake. And it wasn't the first mistake I made about us, either," she added without thinking.

"Oh?" he asked, his voice sounding sarcastic now, almost hurt even. She supposed that was only natural. She'd given him no preparation for this. No reason to suspect that anything was wrong. "There were other mistakes?" he asked further. "Other than marrying me in the first place?"

She nodded again. "Yes. There was another mistake besides that one, too.''

"And what other mistake did you make, Jayne?" he asked coolly.

For one long moment she only looked at him, memorizing his features, imprinting him at the forefront of her brain, so that she could pull out the memory of him later in her life, when he was gone, and remember how wonderful he was. Then, very softly, she said, "I fell in love with you, Erik. And that was my biggest mistake of all.''

And with that she spun on her heel and fled. She didn't think about how she must look running through the parlor with all those curious faces staring after her. She didn't worry about how she was going to get home. And she didn't fret about Chloe or Charlie, whom she knew could fend just fine for themselves among the Randolph clan.

For the first time in her adult life, all Jayne could think about was herself.

And about how empty her life was going to be without Erik.

Eleven

Dinner at Rose Carson's apartment was usually a lively affair, one Jayne, Lila, Meredith and Sylvie enjoyed on a monthly basis. Generally, the four women chattered amiably with their landlady about everything that was going on in their lives, both at work and at play. Tonight, however, the mood was decidedly bleak. Jayne, of course, was still reeling from her conversation with Erik the afternoon before, was still trying to weed through her emotions and figure out exactly what she was feeling. Mostly, though, she just felt numb. And she suspected that would be the case for some time to come.

For now, she had only told Chloe and Charlie that she and Erik had had a quarrel, and that was why she had fled the Randolphs' home the way she had. She could only assume that Erik had told his family something similar, because he hadn't returned to their—her—apartment last night. She hadn't spoken to him since then, but had left a message for him at work that he could come and collect his things this evening, while she was at Rose's having dinner. She hoped he would agree to do that. She wasn't sure she could tolerate having to see him face-to-face again.

In hindsight, Jayne realized that telling her brother and sister that she and Erik had quarreled had been inadvertently convenient. Over the next few months, whenever she spoke to the twins, she could tell them that she and Erik were having problems, and that the two of them weren't getting along. She could explain to her brother and sister that getting married so impulsively, the way they had, had ended up being a bad idea, and that neither of them had been prepared for the massive life changes such a union would bring about. Little by little Jayne could prepare Chloe and Charlie for the inevitable. And maybe, just maybe, it wouldn't be such a devastating blow to them when that inevitable came about.

So Jayne's ruminations over Erik were what had her so quiet and morose tonight. What made the others so quiet and morose was the fact that, earlier at work that day, the rumor of Collette, Inc.'s, hostile takeover had been confirmed. There was indeed someone who was making every effort to buy up stock in the company and force a merger of some kind. Unfortunately, at this point the actual details of the situation were sketchy. No one knew who was trying to hostilely take over the company. And no one knew why.

The general feeling among Collette's employees, however, was that the situation as a whole was not good. As a result, Lila, Sylvie and Meredith were feeling just as lousy as Jayne was tonight, if for entirely different reasons.

"I still wish someone was talking about the particulars of the takeover," Sylvie said from her seat across the table from Jayne. She, like the others, was dressed casually for their dinner, in khaki trousers and a pale-yellow knit top.

"Is no one saying anything?" Rose asked.

Their landlady had been surprisingly curious about the goings-on at Colette, expressing an interest in the takeover that Jayne found unusual. Still, she supposed the whole thing *was* kind of interesting. In a glitzy TV drama sort of way.

"No one's saying much of anything," Jayne told their landlady. "Just that there's definitely someone buying up stock, but no one knows who or why."

"Even some vague reference to the person or persons involved would be helpful at this point," Meredith concurred. She was dressed in her usual colorless, nondescript baggy style. "It's like nobody can find out *any*thing."

Jayne brushed a bread crumb from her sleeveless, white cotton shirt, only to have to flick it from her blue jeans when it landed there. "What about you, Lila?" she asked their other friend, who still wore her work clothes of beige suit and ivory blouse. "You're hooked up higher in the company than we are. Are you hearing anything from your boss?"

"Nicholas?" Lila asked, her voice sounding a little thready for some reason as she spoke the word.

"No, Santa Claus," Sylvie replied sarcastically. "Of course Nicholas. Nicholas Camden. Remember him? He's that yummy VP you work for."

"He *is* yummy, isn't he?" Meredith asked with a giggle.

"Very yummy," Jayne agreed, smiling in spite of her bleak mood.

Each of the women giggled after that. All except for Lila, who reacted by spilling her wine, leaping awkwardly up from her chair, and toppling her plate to the floor in the process. The other women watched with undisguised astonishment as Lila hastily began to clean up the mess. Then they exchanged sidelong glances.

"Why, Lila," Sylvie said as a look of discovery dawned on her face, "whatever is wrong? Was it something we said? Something like, oh…I don't know…about how Nicholas Camden is so yummy?''

Lila was attempting to right her wineglass when Sylvie offered the comment, but at the mention of her boss's name—*thump*—down went the glass again, this time rolling across the table toward Meredith, who scooped it up and set it down without incident.

''Well, well, well,'' Meredith said as she performed the gesture, grinning. ''It would appear that our friend Lila becomes a bit…agitated whenever her boss's name is mentioned. Why is that, Lila, hmmm?''

Lila lifted a hand to brush her hair from her eyes, and Jayne saw that it was trembling ever so slightly. ''I do not get agitated when you say…you know…his name.''

''Whose name?'' Sylvie asked, her own smile rivaling Meredith's. She deliberately waited until Lila was about to set her plate back on the table, then said, ''Nicholas Camden's?''

And *crash* went the plate to the floor again. Muttering a growl of discontent, Lila stooped to pick it up.

''Oh, leave her alone,'' Jayne said, feeling for her friend. Hey, she knew it was no fun to want someone who didn't want you back. ''Stop teasing Lila about Nicholas Camden.''

Thump. This time the sound came from Lila's head as she banged it on the table while trying to rise from the floor.

''Oops,'' Jayne said, genuinely chastened. ''I'm sorry, Lila. I didn't mean to say…you know.''

''Nicholas Camden?'' Meredith tried again.

But this time Lila was ready for it. She only flinched just the tiniest bit in response.

''Oh, Lila,'' Sylvie said in a voice of discovery. ''You've got a thing for your boss. You've got a thing for Nicholas Camden.''

''I do *not*,'' Lila said imperiously. ''have a thing—*any*-thing—for, you know…him.''

Jayne gazed at her friend thoughtfully for a moment, not buying a word of Lila's objection. She really did have a thing for her boss. Oh, my. Between that and the hostile takeover, the next few months should be *very* interesting. Both at Colette and Amber Court.

Rose opened her mouth to say something more, but was halted by a series of quick raps at her front door. She excused herself from the four friends, two of whom continued to needle a third about a certain VP for whom she worked, until Rose returned in a moment with a curious little smile curling her lips.

"It's for you, Jayne," she said softly.

"Me?" Jayne replied, puzzled.

Rose nodded. "It's your husband."

Jayne's eyebrows shot up in surprise. She had told her friends the same thing she'd told Chloe and Charlie—that she and Erik had quarreled and weren't on the best of terms at the moment. She hadn't mentioned to her friends that she had also asked him to move out of 20 Amber Court, but she knew the quarrel story would set the stage, and that she could explain his absence in other ways until the time came to tell everyone they had formally separated.

"I think he wants to apologize for whatever it was the two of you argued about," Rose said.

"But...but...but..." Jayne began. Unfortunately, no more words emerged to help her make sense of the tumult of thoughts wheeling through her brain.

"He certainly looks apologetic, anyway," Rose added, her smile growing broader.

"But..."

"I think you should go talk to him, dear."

"But..."

"He seems a bit...anxious."

Try as she might, Jayne could think of no excuse as to why she shouldn't go and talk to Erik. So, with the other four women gazing expectantly at her, she mumbled, "Excuse me for a minute," and went to see her husband.

Her husband, she thought morosely. Oh, that was a laugh. Funny, though, how laughter was the last response she felt like displaying at the moment.

Erik did indeed look anxious when Jayne poked her head around the corner to gaze down the long corridor toward the front door. He had his hands shoved deep into the pockets of his chocolate-brown trousers, and the buttons of his creamy dress shirt were misaligned, as if he'd been very distracted when he fastened them. His necktie hung around his neck in a careless manner that she'd never known him to display or possess. Erik was generally a satorial wonder, looking as if he'd just stepped out of the pages of *GQ*. At the moment, however, his appearance was obviously the last thing on his mind.

"Hi," he said softly when he saw her.

Jayne moved around the corner of the wall and made her way slowly down the corridor until she stood a scant foot away from him. She noticed then that it wasn't just his clothing that was in uncharacteristic disarray. He'd also obviously not been paying attention when he'd shaved that morning, because dark stubble dotted his jaw and chin. He also had dark circles under his eyes that were unmistakable, as if he'd spent a restless night without sleep. All in all he looked like a man who was deeply troubled by something.

"Hi," she said, just as quietly as he had.

"I, um, I got your message," he told her.

She nodded, crossing her arms over her midsection in a way that felt oddly defensive. "Good," she replied. When he said nothing to elaborate further, she added, "I'll, uh, I'll just wait over here while you get your stuff, if that's okay."

He eyed her thoughtfully for a moment, his dark eyes turbulent. "No," he said. "It's not okay." Then, before she had a chance to comment, he hurried on, "Jayne, we need to talk."

"I think we said everything yesterday that needed to be said," she told him gloomily.

"Oh, no, we didn't," he immediately countered. "We didn't even scrape the tip of the iceberg yesterday."

"What are you talking about?"

He gazed past her, down the corridor, up which drifted feminine laughter and conversation, then back at Jayne. "Can we go down the hall?" he asked.

"To my apartment?" she replied without thinking.

"No, to *our* apartment," he corrected her.

"It's not our apartment anymore," she told him.

He said nothing in response to that, only studied her with a ferocity of intent that she figured she was better off not contemplating. "Can we go down the hall?" he asked again.

She nodded, then strode in that direction, pulling Rose's front door closed behind her. She was about to fish her door key out of her pocket, but Erik already held his in his hand, and he opened the door quickly, gesturing for her to precede him. Jayne did so, performing a perfunctory search for Mojo as she went, so that the ill-tempered cat wouldn't trip her up. There was nothing more humiliating than being felled by a cat when you were about to have—

What? she wondered. Just what was it that she and Erik were about to have? Did he want to go over the details of the breakup the way he had gone over the details of the marriage? Did he want to reiterate that she couldn't file for divorce for twelve months, or else he'd lose $60 million and she'd lose years' worth of college tuition for her brother and sister? As if she needed reminding of those things. The only thing worse than leaving Erik was knowing she'd still be tied to him for twelve months before that break could be made clean.

He followed her into the apartment and closed the door behind them, then traced her steps into the living room.

Jayne had deliberately perched herself on the love seat, thinking Erik would move to the couch, but he joined her instead, seating himself close to her, with scarcely a breath of air separating them. She was about to object, or even move to the couch herself, but Erik took her hand gently in his and began talking.

"Jayne, you can't just tell a man you fell in love with him and then run off the way you did yesterday," he said.

She gazed down at their hands, at the way he was lacing his fingers loosely with hers, as if he weren't even thinking about what he was doing, but was doing it because it was simply a natural gesture on his part. "Why not?" she asked softly.

He said nothing for a moment, not until she turned her gaze back up to his face. Then very quietly he told her, "Because when you run off, it doesn't give the man a chance to respond."

Something fiery and intense flickered to life in his dark eyes then, and an answering blaze erupted in Jayne's belly in response. She was afraid to hope for what she was hoping for, was afraid to ask what she wanted to ask. Nevertheless, "And just how were you planning to respond?" she said, her voice sounding shallow, even to her own ears. Probably, she thought, that was because her breathing was shallow, her thoughts were shallow and, at the moment, anyway, her very perception of reality was shallow.

Erik swallowed visibly, then tightened his fingers with hers. "At first, I wasn't sure how to respond," he told her. "But after spending the last day and night without you, after thinking about the weeks and months to come without you, after visualizing my life ahead without you, now…"

"Now…?" she encouraged him.

"Now I realize…I don't want to live without you."

Jayne held her breath, held his gaze and tried not to

hope. Because he still hadn't said the words she wanted to hear, still hadn't told her what she needed to be told.

"After thinking about all that," he continued, "I know how to respond now." But he said nothing further, only continued to gaze into her eyes as if he couldn't quite believe she was real.

"Then...respond," she told him. "Please respond."

He smiled at that, having detected the urgency in her voice, she supposed. "I love you, too, Jayne," he said simply. "I didn't realize how much until you told me you couldn't stay married to me. Until I realized I was going to lose you. The past few weeks have been the best of my life. I never knew I could feel about anyone the way I feel about you."

"Oh, Erik..."

"I never knew there could be this...this...this satisfaction inside me. This contentment. This knowledge of how everything just feels right with you. And I like that feeling. I like knowing it will always be there."

"Oh, Erik..."

"I married you for money, Jayne," he said softly, covering her hand now with both of his. "But I want to stay with you for something that's worth infinitely more. I want to stay with you because I love you. And I want to stay with you forever."

"Oh, Erik..."

"Is that all you can say?" he asked with a chuckle. "'Oh, Erik'?"

"Oh, Erik..." she said once more, laughing with him.

"Tell me again," he said. "Tell me how...you know."

"I love you?" she asked.

He nodded. "Yes, that."

"I love you," she told him.

"Forever?"

"Forever."

"And you won't leave?"

She shook her head and smiled. "No. Never. You're stuck with me now."

"Even after twelve months is up?"

"Even after twelve months is up."

"Even when Chloe and Charlie graduate with their Ph.D.s?"

"Even then."

He smiled again, looking a little less anxious than he had before. Then he released her hand and shoved one of his into his trouser pocket. He extracted a small, square box and flipped it open, to reveal her wedding and engagement rings within. Silently he withdrew them, then, as Jayne watched silently, he took her left hand in his and slid first one, then the other back where they had been before. Back where they belonged.

"I do love you," he told her again, squeezing her fingers gently, possessively.

"And I'll never get tired of hearing that," she told him.

"I hope you never get tired of saying it, either."

She grinned. "I love you, Erik."

He grinned back. "That's what I like to hear."

He leaned forward then and covered her mouth with his, kissing her softly, sweetly, chastely. Right now wasn't the time for passion, but for promise. The passion, Jayne knew, would come later. Like maybe in an hour or so. Fifteen minutes, if they kept going the way they were now. At the moment, however, she only wanted to tell him, in so many ways, how much she loved, wanted and needed him. And she wanted him to tell her, in so many ways, the same thing.

For long moments they only sat on the love seat, hand in hand, kissing, caressing, loving, promising. Then Erik released her hand and trailed his fingers up along her bare arm, over her shoulder, along the collar of her shirt, then down lower, toward her breast. As his hand drifted down, he skimmed his fingers over the amber brooch Rose had loaned Jayne nearly a month ago and which she still wore.

She remembered then that she had meant to return it earlier, at dinner. Somehow, though, she'd gotten a bit sidetracked before she had the chance. Now she leaped up from the love seat and began to unfasten it.

"What are you doing?" Erik asked. "We were just getting to the good part."

Jayne smiled. "I have to do something before I forget."

Erik grinned lasciviously and patted the cushion she had just vacated. "Hey, I can make you forget anything. Just give me another minute or two."

"That's the problem," she told him. "And I need to give this back to Rose before you turn my brain into pudding." She unhooked the brooch, then cradled it carefully in one hand. "You are planning to turn my brain into pudding this evening, aren't you?"

"Oh, baby. You can count on it."

She grinned. "Then I'll definitely hurry back."

"You'd better."

Erik's seductive laughter hastened Jayne's speed as she jogged to her own front door, then to Rose's, where she rapped quickly three times.

"Hi, Rose," Jayne said as her landlady opened the front door. "I forgot to give this back to you earlier." She extended the amber brooch, still cupped gingerly in her palm. "I apologize. I didn't mean to keep your pin for as long as I did."

Rose smiled as she took the proffered brooch and cradled it gently in the palm of her own hand. Very softly she ran the pad of her index finger over each of the amber inserts, as if they were the most precious gems in the world. And Jayne supposed that in a way they were. At least to Rose Carson.

"Oh, that's all right, dear," the older woman said. "I wanted you to wear it for as long as you needed it. I thought it might bring you a lift."

Now Jayne was the one to smile. "Oh, it did do that," she assured her landlady. She glanced over her shoulder, toward Erik, who stood framed in her own doorway, as if he hadn't wanted to let her out of his sight. Then she turned her attention back to Rose. "And it brought me a lot more than a lift, too."

Jayne expected the other woman to look puzzled in light of the cryptic statement, but Rose only smiled knowingly, as if she understood completely. In response, though, she only said, "Perhaps I'll loan the brooch to Lila for a little while. After all the teasing she's endured tonight over Nicholas Camden, I think she could use a lift, too." Rose's blue eyes sparkled as she added, "Among other things."

Jayne figured she probably managed a little twinkle of her own as she replied, "Thanks again for the loan, Rose. Somehow, though, I think I can take things from here myself."

Her landlady turned her gaze first from Jayne, then to Erik, then back to Jayne again. "Oh, I don't doubt that for a moment," she said. "I'd say the two of you together can handle just about anything."

"Thanks, Rose," Jayne said again. "For everything."

"And thanks from me, too," Erik called from down the hall. He did sound a bit puzzled, though, as he added, "For…whatever."

Rose glanced at the amber brooch one last time before lifting her other hand to Jayne and Erik in farewell. Then she closed the door, leaving the newlyweds alone in the hallway outside.

"So what do you say?" Jayne asked her husband as she entered her apartment again. She halted in front of Erik, then circled her arms around his neck. "Since we're starting this marriage over, you think we ought to give that honeymoon thing a second go-around, too?"

Erik nodded. "Oh, yes. But this time we're going to do things the right way."

Jayne arched her eyebrows in speculation. "Oh? I thought they went pretty well the first time."

"This time," he said, "it will be even better."

"Now that's a promise I look forward to you keeping," she told him with a smile.

Erik smiled, too, then surprised her by scooping her up into his arms. So astonished was she, in fact, that all she could do in response was tighten her hold on him and laugh.

"I never carried you over the threshold the first time," he told her.

She thought about that for a moment, then nodded. "That's true. You didn't."

"So I'm going to start with that," he said.

"But I'm already inside," she pointed out unnecessarily.

"That's okay," he said. "We're not staying."

"We're not?"

He shook his head. "We have places to go, things to do, people to meet. We have our whole lives ahead of us."

She thought about that for a moment, then realized she couldn't wait to get started. "Wow. You're right."

"So what do you say, Jayne? Will you marry me again? The right way this time? For the right reasons?"

"Oh, yes. I will. I do," she said, hastily correcting herself.

Now Erik was the one to laugh. "I do, too. And I will. Just as soon as we get where we're going."

"And just where is it we're going?" she asked him.

He smiled. "I don't know. But it's going to be a wonderful journey getting there."

"It will be," she agreed. "I know it will."

And with that, Erik covered Jayne's mouth with his and carried her over the threshold, *out* of her apartment, and into their life together.

* * * * *

*Turn the page for a sneak preview
of the next* 20 AMBER COURT *title,
SOME KIND OF INCREDIBLE
by popular author Kathy Garbera
on sale in October 2001
from Silhouette Desire...
And don't miss any of the books in the*
20 AMBER COURT *series,
only from Silhouette Desire:*

WHEN JAYNE MET ERIK,
September 2001
by Elizabeth Bevarly

SOME KIND OF INCREDIBLE,
October 2001
by Kathy Garbera

THE BACHELORETTE,
November 2001
by Kate Little

RISQUÉ BUSINESS,
December 2001
by Anne Marie Winston

One

Late again, Lila Maxwell thought as she hurried to close the door to her third-floor apartment. She loved her home. It wasn't much, a four-room apartment in an older but nicely kept building. She'd spent the last two years carefully decorating each part until her flat of rooms had become her dream home.

She hurried down the stairs, noticing the dark morning, and longing, just for a minute, for the warmth of her native Florida. Youngsville, Indiana, had a great community, but the weather was sometimes too cold for this Florida girl.

"Lila, can you stop for a cup of coffee?"

"Rose, I wish I could, but Nick's due back from his business trip today and I'd like to be in the office before he gets there." Nicholas Camden was her boss. And the man of her dreams.

Not girlish fantasies she'd entertained of a white knight that rescued her from the small government subsidized duplex she and her mother had shared. But womanly fantasies of dark passion with a man who saw her for more than a nice collection of body parts. She flushed a little and hoped Rose didn't notice.

"I have something for you. Wait here a minute," Rose said.

Lila loved her landlady. She was kind and caring and made her feel at home when everything around her was foreign.

"Here it is, Lila."

Rose handed her a beautiful piece of jewelry. A brooch made of amber and precious metal. It was almost heart-shaped and, though the term seemed inappropriate in the presence of something so unique, it was pretty. As Lila fingered it gently, she knew she'd never allow herself to wear it. "I can't take this."

She handed it back to Rose, but the woman refused to take it.

"Just borrow it for luck."

"Thank you, Rose, but no. This is too valuable."

"I want you to wear it. It needs to be on a pretty young lady."

Rose brushed aside Lila's coat and fastened the brooch to her suit jacket. Lila tried to remove it, but Rose's hand covered hers.

"Lila, it would mean a lot to me. It brought Mitch and me together. I like to think it brings love to the lives of those it touches."

Rose got that misty look she always did when she spoke of her deceased husband. Unwilling to upset her landlady, Lila decided to keep the brooch for today and return it tonight.

"Thanks, Rose. It is lovely. I have to go," Lila said with a glance of her watch.

Rose nodded, and Lila hurried out into the cold. The sun was breaking over the horizon. It was nippy but not too cold for a walk to work. She lifted her face to the sun and pretended the high for today was fifty degrees.

She loved the long park and trees that were filled with fall colors. Yellows, browns, oranges and reds filled every space. Halloween, her favorite holiday, was right around the corner, she thought, attributing the extra bounce in her step of excitement.

Usually she had some company on her walks to work. Sometimes Jayne and Sylvie walked with her, but Jayne had recently gotten married and hadn't been up so early in the mornings. And today she was up and out too early for Sylvie and Meredith.

Lila liked the fact that she had good friends here. It was as if she'd found the surrogate family she'd always been searching for. She really loved her life here in Youngsville.

A car slowed behind her. The low purr of an expensive engine told her it wasn't one of the other Colette, Inc., secretaries offering her a ride. She kept her head down and walked. Out of the corner of her eye she could see Nick's sporty coup following her. But she wasn't prepared to face Nick outside the office.

Men only want one thing from women like us, Lila. Her mother's warning echoed in her mind. And she didn't glance over despite the warmth emanating from the open window.

"Want a lift, Lila?"

"No, thanks, I'm enjoying the crisp morning." If only she could stop shivering.

"Liar," he said, not unkindly.

He was right, she was lying. But that didn't mean she was going to admit it. Lila wasn't getting in the car with him, because after last week she didn't trust herself. She'd spent all of her time in Indiana adjusting to the new community and her home, learning to be proficient at her job and making some friends. But she hadn't been prepared for Nick Camden when he turned his sexy gaze her way.

She'd dreamed of him kissing her and touching her, but when he'd leaned closer to her last week in the office, she'd frozen. Paralyzed with fear that she would disappoint him, she'd backed away. Still he'd had a gleam in his eye that said retreat wasn't possible.

But two years ago she'd decided that Indiana was a place for fresh starts. She wasn't going to get involved with any man unless she knew for certain that it was right. Which meant no Nick Camden. No matter how fast he made her blood run.

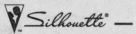

Feel like a star with Silhouette.

We will fly you and a guest to New York City for an exciting weekend stay at a glamorous 5-star hotel. Experience a refreshing day at one of New York's trendiest spas and have your photo taken by a professional. Plus, receive $1,000 U.S. spending money!

Flowers...long walks...dinner for two... how does Silhouette Books make romance come alive for you?

Send us a script, with 500 words or less, along with visuals (only drawings, magazine cutouts or photographs or combination thereof). Show us how Silhouette Makes Your Love Come Alive. Be creative and have fun. No purchase necessary. All entries must be clearly marked with your name, address and telephone number. All entries will become property of Silhouette and are not returnable. **Contest closes September 28, 2001.**

Please send your entry to: **Silhouette Makes You a Star!**

In U.S.A.	In Canada
P.O. Box 9069	P.O. Box 637
Buffalo, NY, 14269-9069	Fort Erie, ON, L2A 5X3

Look for contest details on the next page, by visiting www.eHarlequin.com or request a copy by sending a self-addressed envelope to the applicable address above. Contest open to Canadian and U.S. residents who are 18 or over. Void where prohibited.

Where love comes alive™

Our lucky winner's photo will appear in a Silhouette ad. Join the fun!

HARLEQUIN "SILHOUETTE MAKES YOU A STAR!" CONTEST 1308
OFFICIAL RULES
NO PURCHASE NECESSARY TO ENTER

1. To enter, follow directions published in the offer to which you are responding. Contest begins June 1, 2001, and ends on September 28, 2001. Entries must be postmarked by September 28, 2001, and received by October 5, 2001. Enter by hand-printing (or typing) on an 8 ½" x 11" piece of paper your name, address (including zip code), contest number/name and attaching a script containing 500 words or less, along with drawings, photographs or magazine cutouts, or combinations thereof (i.e., collage) on no larger than 9" x 12" piece of paper, describing how the Silhouette books make romance come alive for you. Mail via first-class mail to: Harlequin "Silhouette Makes You a Star!" Contest 1308, (in the U.S.) P.O. Box 9069, Buffalo, NY 14269-9069, (in Canada) P.O. Box 637, Fort Erie, Ontario, Canada L2A 5X3. Limit one entry per person, household or organization.

2. Contests will be judged by a panel of members of the Harlequin editorial, marketing and public relations staff. Fifty percent of criteria will be judged against script and fifty percent will be judged against drawing, photographs and/or magazine cutouts. Judging criteria will be based on the following:

    - Sincerity—25%
    - Originality and Creativity—50%
    - Emotionally Compelling—25%

   In the event of a tie, duplicate prizes will be awarded. Decisions of the judges are final.

3. All entries become the property of Torstar Corp. and may be used for future promotional purposes. Entries will not be returned. No responsibility is assumed for lost, late, illegible, incomplete, inaccurate, nondelivered or misdirected mail.

4. Contest open only to residents of the U.S. (except Puerto Rico) and Canada who are 18 years of age or older, and is void wherever prohibited by law; all applicable laws and regulations apply. Any litigation within the Province of Quebec respecting the conduct or organization of a publicity contest may be submitted to the Régie des alcools, des courses et des jeux for a ruling. Any litigation respecting the awarding of a prize may be submitted to the Régie des alcools, des courses et des jeux only for the purpose of helping the parties reach a settlement. Employees and immediate family members of Torstar Corp. and D. L. Blair, Inc., their affiliates, subsidiaries and all other agencies, entities and persons connected with the use, marketing or conduct of this contest are not eligible to enter. Taxes on prizes are the sole responsibility of the winner. Acceptance of any prize offered constitutes permission to use winner's name, photograph or other likeness for the purposes of advertising, trade and promotion on behalf of Torstar Corp., its affiliates and subsidiaries without further compensation to the winner, unless prohibited by law.

5. Winner will be determined no later than November 30, 2001, and will be notified by mail. Winner will be required to sign and return an Affidavit of Eligibility/Release of Liability/Publicity Release form within 15 days after winner notification. Noncompliance within that time period may result in disqualification and an alternative winner may be selected. All travelers must execute a Release of Liability prior to ticketing and must possess required travel documents (e.g., passport, photo ID) where applicable. Trip must be booked by December 31, 2001, and completed within one year of notification. No substitution of prize permitted by winner. Torstar Corp. and D. L. Blair, Inc., their parents, affiliates and subsidiaries are not responsible for errors in printing of contest, entries and/or game pieces. In the event of printing or other errors that may result in unintended prize values or duplication of prizes, all affected game pieces or entries shall be null and void. **Purchase or acceptance of a product offer does not improve your chances of winning.**

6. Prizes: (1) Grand Prize—A 2-night/3-day trip for two (2) to New York City, including round-trip coach air transportation nearest winner's home and hotel accommodations (double occupancy) at The Plaza Hotel, a glamorous afternoon makeover at a trendy New York spa, $1,000 in U.S. spending money and an opportunity to have a professional photo taken and appear in a Silhouette advertisement (approximate retail value: $7,000). (10) Ten Runner-Up Prizes of gift packages (retail value $50 ea.). Prizes consist of only those items listed as part of the prize. Limit one prize per person. Prize is valued in U.S. currency.

7. For the name of the winner (available after December 31, 2001) send a self-addressed, stamped envelope to: Harlequin "Silhouette Makes You a Star!" Contest 1197 Winners, P.O. Box 4200 Blair, NE 68009-4200 or you may access the www.eHarlequin.com Web site through February 28, 2002.

Contest sponsored by Torstar Corp., P.O. Box 9042, Buffalo, NY 14269-9042.

SRMYAS2

If you enjoyed what you just read,
then we've got an offer you can't resist!

Take 2 bestselling love stories FREE!

Plus get a FREE surprise gift!

In September 2001,

SILHOUETTE *Silhouette*

SPECIAL EDITION™

presents the final book in

DIANA PALMER's

exciting new *Soldiers of Fortune* trilogy:

THE
LAST MERCENARY

(SE #1417)

Traveling far and wide to rescue Callie Kirby from a dangerous
desperado was far less daunting for Micah Steele than trying to
combat his potent desire for the virginal beauty. For the heavenly
taste of Callie's sweetly tempting lips was slowly driving Micah
insane. Was the last mercenary *finally* ready to claim his bride?

Don't miss any of the adventurous
SOLDIERS OF FORTUNE *tales from*
international bestselling author Diana Palmer!

MERCENARY'S WOMAN, SR #1444
THE WINTER SOLDIER, SD #1351
THE LAST MERCENARY, SE #1417

Soldiers of Fortune...prisoners of love.

Available only from Silhouette Books at your favorite retail outlet.

Silhouette®
Where love comes alive™

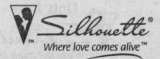